The characters and events portrayed in this book are fictitious. Any similarity to real persons, living or dead, is coincidental and not intended by the author. Any reference to real locations is only for atmospheric effect, and in no way truly represents those locations.

Copyright © 2023 by Ryan Casey

Cover design by Miblart

All rights reserved.

No part of this book may be reproduced in any form or by any electronic or mechanical means, including information storage and retrieval systems, without written permission from the author, except for the use of brief quotations in a book review.

Published by Higher Bank Books

GET A POST APOCALYPTIC NOVEL FOR FREE

To instantly receive an exclusive post apocalyptic novel totally free, sign up for Ryan Casey's author newsletter at: ryancaseybooks.com/fanclub

CARLY

* * *

Carly Harper woke up on Wednesday, August 4th, expecting an entirely ordinary day until she saw the blood smeared all over the quilt cover.

Her first reaction? Faint irritation. This bedding was her favourite. All white, with a few blue petals trickled across it. It was very "zen". She liked the style so much that she got two, so she could immediately cover the bed in the same print while the other was being washed. A little bit obsessive, perhaps. But Carly was always very particular.

And seeing the blood smeared across her bed right now... Carly wondered if she was a terrible person. Because instead of worrying about the welfare of the person who must be bleeding right now—or even worrying whether the blood was her own—it was her damned bedding she was thinking of.

She heard shuffling. A thump outside her bedroom. Something heavy, hitting the floor. Like someone was out there. Struggling. Shit. Her heart started to race. Her body filled with heat.

Again, she knew it made her awful, but her first fear wasn't for the welfare of the woman outside her room.

It was for herself.

Because this blood. It was a lot of blood.

And this blood.

This blood wasn't her blood.

It was the woman's blood.

And the woman wasn't just any normal lover.

The blood belonged to a sex worker.

Which complicated things.

She sat there in bed, frozen solid. The air was thick and stuffy. She was covered in sweat. She hated the feeling when it stuck her legs together. When it made the damp bedsheets cling to her skin. The smell of sweat in the air.

And the rusty smell of *blood*, too.

She listened to the shuffling on the landing, and her heart raced. She couldn't move a muscle. The woman. The woman out there was an escort. She wasn't supposed to keep ordering escorts in. She just... found it difficult. Found it difficult, living alone. Found it hard enough connecting with people. Sometimes, she downloaded apps. But the people looking for short-term connections didn't interest her. It was the ones looking for longer-term that interested her. Because it was that potential. It was that spark. That connection. That's what made the sex light up.

But inevitably, after talking to them, after going for drinks with them, after talking about future life plans that she so dearly *wanted* to explore... she'd sleep with them. The connection would be strong, and the intimacy would be strong, and then... well, after that, it was too close. It was far too close.

So she'd cut things off. Coldly. She'd block. She'd ghost completely.

And occasionally, those people she'd used and discarded would find a way to contact her. Or they'd bump into her in town. And when they did, they'd lambast her. They'd shout at her. Tell her she was a piece of shit.

And in a way, that made her feel better for ditching them. Because if they were going apeshit on a woman they barely knew—okay, sometimes seven or eight dates followed by passionate sex—then they definitely weren't stable enough for a future. They weren't mentally okay. That's what she kept telling herself.

But the ones who just looked at her got to her most.

Looked at her with these pale faces.

With these dead eyes.

A look of distance, where previously, she'd seen a spark. Previously, she'd seen hope. Previously, she'd even seen blossoming love.

And in its place...

Emptiness.

Deadness.

Like an infection.

And she was the cause.

She heard the rustling outside her bedroom, and she felt sick. This was a nightmare. It had to be a nightmare. The blood on the sheets. The struggling outside the door. If something had happened with a sex worker in her presence... what would that mean for her?

And was it so selfish to think that way?

She remembered the first time she contacted an escort. Online, on one of the more established websites. She told them she wanted to pretend they were building up a connection. That they were getting to know each other. That they were getting close. That they were in the throes of a developing relationship. That they'd go on a few nice dates, out for drinks, for meals, cute shit like that.

And then they'd get closer. And eventually, they'd sleep together.

And the beauty with the escorts?

They didn't care if she went AWOL for weeks after they'd slept together.

As long as Carly was clean and she paid nicely, they didn't care whatsoever.

But this one...

The girl was called LizzyX69. That's how Carly knew her. She slept with men and women, sometimes at the same time. She had no limits, apparently. And although Carly wasn't willing to test those limits, she believed her from some of the videos she'd seen on her profile. Stuff she didn't even want to elaborate on.

But Carly didn't really want to test any of her limits. She wasn't interested in any taboos. Or anything like that.

The only thing she was interested in?

Building a fake connection with this girl.

And then sleeping with her—making *love* to her.

And tonight was the night.

The sex was passionate. It was close. But the moans LizzyX69 was making. There was something off about them. There was something *false* about them.

And it didn't help that she couldn't stop sniffing.

Full of a cold.

A cold that seemed to be progressing rapidly as the night went on.

But Carly looked past it. They had great sex. And then they fell to sleep together, bodies close, arms wrapped around each other.

And for a moment, for just a moment, Carly felt that closeness; she felt that warmth, and she imagined it was real. She imagined it was the first night of many nights. The first night of the rest of her life.

And then a tear rolled down her cheek.

Because she knew it wouldn't last.

She knew it could never last.

Because she didn't deserve anyone.

She didn't deserve love.

She heard LizzyX69 struggling along the landing area of her home, and she took a deep breath of the clammy, bloody air.

She couldn't just lie here.

She couldn't be so fucking selfish as to only think about herself.

She had to get up.

She had to see if this girl was okay.

She climbed out of the blood-soaked bed. She walked across the plush carpet. Patches of blood contrasted with the dark grey. Shit. Her new carpet, too. She felt the warmth of it beneath her feet and saw how thick and so dark those stains were, and she knew she was never, ever going to get those out of the carpet.

She stood at the bedroom door. She felt her heart racing. She pictured finding LizzyX69 lying in a heap on the landing floor. A brain aneurysm? Some kind of haemorrhage? Fuck. Whatever it was, it wasn't good.

She gulped. She lifted her shaking hand. Grabbed the handle and held it. Tight.

It'll be okay. Everything is going to be okay. This isn't a nightmare. It's real life. And everything's going to be okay.

She lowered the bloody handle and pulled open the door.

She saw more blood. Blood on the beige carpet outside the bedroom.

Handprints of blood. Smeared across the white banister.

And she could *hear* something.

Shuffling.

Shuffling, just out of sight.

Like someone was *dragging* themselves across her landing.

She stood there.

Shaking.

Teeth chattering against each other.

Keep calm, Carly. You've got this. Everything is going to be okay.

She lifted her shaking foot. It felt so heavy. She could barely lift it. Barely move it. She was so captured. By fear.

She stepped further out of the room. And she could *hear* that shuffling now.

So close.

To her right.

Right beside her.

She stood there.

Jaw tensing up.

She gulped.

She took a deep breath, the smell of her own skin still strong in the air.

Come on, Carly. You have to do this. You have to.

And then she turned around.

LizzyX69 was lying on the landing. She was on her knees. She was completely naked. Her legs were covered in tattoos. And her blonde hair was dangling down the back of her neck.

It was peppered with blood.

She was heaving. Vomiting blood. All over the landing floor.

And all Carly's worry about her own carpet was gone now.

All her fear about the condition of her home was gone.

All she cared about was LizzyX69.

But she was scared, too.

"Lizzy," Carly said. Her voice breaking. Shaking. Quivering.

Lizzy didn't move. She just lay there on her shaking knees. Vomiting.

And outside, Carly could hear all kinds of noises. Sirens. She could hear what sounded like… cars. Colliding.

And she swore she could hear screaming.

But she couldn't focus on it. Not properly.

The only thing she could focus on was the woman heaving onto her carpet.

The only thing she could focus on was the blood.

Spewing from her lips.

The only thing she could focus on was this poor, sick woman

right in front of her.

"Lizzy," she said. Realising that her name probably wasn't even Lizzy at all. "Are you..."

Suddenly, Lizzy's head shot up.

She turned around.

Slowly.

And then she looked at Carly with these... these dead eyes.

The dead eyes that reminded her of the women she'd used.

The women she'd ghosted.

The souls she'd broken.

Dead.

She stood there. Shaking. Staring down at Lizzy.

Blood oozing from her chapped, gnawed lips.

Trickling from her eyes and from her ears.

Smeared in her hair.

She looked down at her, and she knew what she needed to do.

She needed to call an ambulance.

She needed to get her to hospital.

She was sick. Very sick.

And no matter what her own worries were... she needed to help her.

"Lizzy," she said. Head spinning as she took another step towards her. "We need to..."

And then something unexpected happened.

Lizzy opened her mouth and let out this low, rumbling growl.

She sounded... like a monster. Like a feral animal.

Crouched there.

Crouched there, covered in blood.

And looking at her with these dead eyes.

But also with this *anger*.

"Lizzy," Carly gasped. "What's..."

And then something else unpredictable happened.

Something else unexpected.

Lizzy leaped up.

She tackled Carly to the floor.

Carly screamed.

She screamed as blood splattered from Lizzy's mouth and all over her.

She kicked out and punched out and tried to get her off her, tried to get her away.

But Lizzy kept her pinned down.

She was only a small woman. But she had a strength. A strength that went beyond her body. Beyond her size.

"Help!" Carly screamed, realising how fucking pathetic she sounded. "Please. Please…"

And then something else happened.

She couldn't explain it.

She couldn't understand it.

She couldn't comprehend it.

But Lizzy wrapped her teeth around Carly's arm.

And then she sunk her teeth down into her flesh.

Hard.

A burning pain split through Carly's arm. She screamed. She kicked out. She punched out. She did everything she could.

Everything to try and get her off.

Everything to try and loosen her grip.

She looked down at Lizzy.

Teeth clamped around her arm.

Blood oozing out of her arm.

Greyed-out eyes rolling back into her head in the same way they did last night when she was having an orgasm that Carly knew was probably fake.

Blood spluttered from her flesh.

Her sharp canines dug further into her skin.

"Please," Carly said. "Please…"

And then, without even thinking, she grabbed whatever she could find in her reach—a heavy metal ornament beside the side table.

She grabbed it.

And she swung it at Lizzy's head.

Hard.

She hit.

And she kept on hitting.

She kept on hitting, just trying to release her, just trying to get her off her, just trying to break free.

But Lizzy stayed clamped on.

Lizzy kept on biting.

"Please!" Carly said. Tears streaming down her face.

She hit harder.

And harder.

So hard, blood splattered out of her skull.

Dripped from her hair.

And she kept going until her skull cracked, and even then, she was still clamped on.

"Please," Carly said. "Please…"

She wasn't sure how many times she cracked that ornament against Lizzy's head.

But eventually, she finally loosened her grip on Carly's arm.

Her body slumped, twitching, to the landing floor.

Blood oozed out of her skull.

Covering her beige carpet.

Carly sat there.

Shaking.

Clinging the ornament in her grip.

Watching the blood ooze out in a puddle all around her.

She sat there shaking.

She sat there holding her bleeding arm.

She sat there, sweat pouring down her face.

Shaking.

"Please," Carly said as she held on to her arm, the sound of sirens ringing outside her house. "Please. Please…"

KEIRA

* * *

Keira saw the charred bodies lying in the road.
And the scariest thing?
She didn't feel anything anymore.
There were four of them. Lying together. Huddled together. It looked like a family. A father, a mother. Two children.

Lying there on the road. Their skin blackened and burned. Their mouths outstretched in terror. The smell of burned meat clinging to her nostrils.

She looked down at those bodies, and she wanted to believe they were infected when they died. But there was no knowing. And besides. There was no knowing whether the infected felt any pain. There was no knowing what they might go through when they were attacked, either. It certainly *seemed* like they were enraged. Like they were different people than they were before. Almost like they were possessed with rage.

But what if they were just ordinary people inside those bodies?

What if their old selves remained locked in the worst kind of locked-in syndrome and forced to commit the horrors they were responsible for?

She couldn't know. How could anyone ever know? There was only one way of knowing. And that was by being bitten. By turning. Becoming infected.

Keira didn't plan on being bitten any time soon.

Finding out any time soon.

She looked down at those bodies, and she just felt this... emptiness. This void. Deep inside her chest.

Because they were just another set of bodies.

Another reminder of death.

Another reminder of loss.

She thought about all the bodies she'd seen over the last few weeks. She thought about the men she'd seen. The women she'd seen. The children she'd seen. She thought about the dogs she'd seen, wandering lonely down the road, forlorn, emaciated. She saw the empty cars. The smashed windows. She heard the crows cawing, echoing all around her. And she thought about how even the smallest of sounds gathered her attention.

Because the smallest of sounds could be a sign.

A sign of the infected.

A sign that they were close.

And then she thought of Dad.

Her stomach turned when she thought of Dad. When she pictured his final moments.

Sitting there beside her.

Holding her hand.

Turning. Succumbing to the infection.

She wondered what he'd witnessed in his final moments.

She wondered whether he'd still been conscious. Still been aware.

She wondered whether he would've been disappointed with her for letting him turn.

She took a deep breath of the smoky air.

Swallowed a thick lump in her throat.

She did all she could for Dad.

And she would keep doing all she could for the people she cared about.

She heard footsteps beside her. Approaching her. The sound of hard nails on the road. She turned around and saw Rufus wandering along beside her. Wagging his tail. That look of contentedness on his face. Almost like a smile.

And honestly, it broke her. Seeing him lowering his ears, wagging his tail, panting away.

He was still so happy.

He was still so content.

Even though everything around him was crumbling to shit.

Even though he wasn't eating anywhere near as frequently. None of them were. He'd lost weight. She could see his ribs now.

She stroked his bony head. Felt his fur under her fingertips. Saw his big brown eyes staring up at her with such trust. With such faith.

She hoped she could repay that faith. She hoped she was worth the faith he was putting in her.

She saw more movement in the corner of her eyes, and the hairs on the back of her neck stood on end.

When she looked up, she saw Nisha. Nisha had lost weight, too. She wasn't the biggest girl to begin with. But she'd crept over the edge into being underweight, by the looks of things. Which, in this world, was a dangerous place to be.

She didn't have the same glow in her eyes.

The same happiness on her face.

She looked pale. She walked with slumped shoulders. She used to be a quick walker, especially when they first met.

But since leaving the bunker three days ago—since beginning this journey towards the North Lancs barracks, which was supposedly a well-populated safe haven with an *antidote*—something had changed in Nisha.

Keira remembered the bunker. She remembered Kevin. She remembered him standing there as the infected surrounded him.

And she remembered the note Nisha left her when she woke from unconsciousness.

I've done something bad.

She shivered when she remembered those words. The look of panic on Nisha's face when she'd walked over to her, sitting there in the darkness. Sheer panic. Pure horror.

And then the denial.

The outright denial, the moment they'd stepped out of the bunker.

Asking Nisha the question.

Do you know anything about what happened to Kevin's people in the bunker?

The hesitation on Nisha's face.

The way she glanced up at Keira like she so desperately wanted to tell her something but couldn't.

And then the way she so definitively wrote on the piece of paper: *No.*

Keira looked down at Nisha as she walked to her side.

You okay? Keira signed. She wasn't sure if she was getting it completely right. But she was trying her best.

Nisha glanced up at her. It took her a few seconds to react. Almost as if she wasn't registering Keira's signing at first.

She looked into Keira's eyes. Right into her eyes. That dead-eyed stare. A dead-eyed stare that...

No.

She didn't want to admit it.

But she couldn't fight it.

A dead-eyed stare that reminded her of the infected.

She stood there. Looking down at Nisha. This girl. Bitten. A girl with the ability to repel the infected. A girl with the ability to do God knows whatever else.

She looked right into Keira's eyes.

And then, finally, she nodded.

And then she looked away from Keira and walked right past her.

Keira watched Nisha walk past her.

She watched Rufus cower the second she walked by.

Saw his hackles raise.

Heard him growl.

She swallowed a lump in her throat as they stood on this abandoned road towards the North Lancs barracks.

She watched Nisha walking by.

Past the charred bodies.

She didn't even look at them as she walked by them.

It was as if something had changed in her.

Something had transformed inside her.

Something had broken inside her.

And it scared Keira just where it might lead next.

Then she remembered Jean.

She remembered Omar.

She remembered Dad.

And she remembered the promise she'd made to all of them.

She was going to protect Nisha.

Because that was her duty.

She took a deep breath.

She gulped down another sickly lump in her throat.

And then she walked after Nisha, after Rufus, and past the charred bodies on the concrete, as the rain trickled down from the cloudy sky above…

NISHA

***

Nisha didn't feel alive anymore.

She could see the road ahead of her. She could see the cars sitting there in the middle of the street. She could see the smashed glass and feel it crunching beneath her feet.

And she could see the bodies, too.

The burned bodies lying in the road.

It looked like a man, a woman, and two children. She always wanted a sister. But Dad and Mum never wanted another one because Mum was always drinking or angry. And then, when Mum left, Dad didn't want to meet another woman. He just wanted to look after Nisha. That's what he said.

Even though she wanted him to meet someone nice.

Someone who... wasn't *Mum*. But who could make Dad happy. And could look after her like Mum used to, too.

She could smell burning in the air. It made her feel sick. It reminded her of the smell of meat at a barbecue. The school barbecue in the summertime. The one Dad took her to. She was looking forward to it for so many days because they had a bouncy slide there, and she was really looking forward to going on the bouncy slide.

But when she got there, hand in hand with Dad, she saw a load of the other kids from her year. Only they weren't with their parents. They were on their own.

And they were laughing at her. Laughing at her and sniggering at her to each other. And she felt her cheeks heating up, her face burning, and suddenly, she didn't feel like going on the bouncy slide so much anymore.

Dad asked her why she didn't fancy it. She shook her head. But she saw him looking up, then. Over at the other kids, who were laughing at her.

He asked her if she wanted to go for ice cream somewhere else. She nodded. In the car on the way to the ice cream place, she tried her best not to cry. She wished she was normal. She wished she wasn't deaf. And as much as she loved Dad, she wished she was strong and brave enough to go places without him.

Only... that wasn't really true, was it?

Because Dad was Nisha's best friend.

And she wanted to go everywhere with him.

He pulled up somewhere she didn't recognise. She didn't see any ice cream vans anywhere. Or anything like that. But he nudged her. Nudged her on the arm and pointed ahead. And she saw the rollercoaster towering over her.

She saw it, and she smiled, and she hugged him tight. A theme park. He'd taken her to a theme park.

And as she held him tight, squeezed him, she realised at that moment that she didn't need friends. She didn't need a stupid school barbecue. She didn't need anyone.

She only needed Dad.

She stood in the middle of the road and looked around at Rufus. He was looking up at her with the hairs on his back raised. With his tail down, between his legs. His teeth were showing.

And he didn't look her in the eye properly. He looked like he was growling.

She looked up at Keira, then. Saw the way she looked down at her. She usually smiled at her right away. Like Dad used to.

But she didn't smile right away at her now.

She looked at her with wide eyes.

Like she was scared.

And that made Nisha feel sad, too. Because she knew why Keira was looking at her that way. But there was nothing she could do about it. Nothing she could do about it at all.

She thought back to the bunker place.

She thought back to the voice in her head.

The voice telling her to open the door.

Then telling her to give everyone up.

And then…

The man. The one Keira called Kevin.

She wasn't sure how she spoke to the voice. But she told the voice she was going to give Kevin to them.

And when she'd given Kevin to them… the bad people were happy.

For now.

The *voice* was happy for now.

She stood there, shaking. She couldn't tell Keira what she'd done. Because if she told her that, she'd think she was crazy. Or worse—she'd think she was a monster.

But it didn't matter what she did and didn't tell Keira. She knew something was wrong anyway. She'd seen it. She'd seen Nisha hold bad people back before. She'd seen how they'd walked out of that room; those two and Rufus, and the bad people didn't hurt them. They didn't touch them at all.

And then she'd seen the bad people all turn on the man called Kevin and swarm him.

Nisha gulped. Her heart raced. She didn't know what she'd done. She didn't really know how she'd done it.

But she knew she'd done the only thing she could to help her, Keira, and Rufus out of that place.

She thought about what Keira had told her when they got out. About her dad, David. And about Sarah, too. They were gone. They were both gone.

And Nisha felt sad at first. Because she liked David. And even though Sarah was weird, she liked her too.

But now, she felt... nothing.

She felt nothing at all.

She stood there in the middle of the road and thought of the only thing that made her feel anything.

The Girl.

She hadn't seen The Girl in a while. She was beginning to wonder whether she was even real at all. Or if she was just a part of her mind.

But when she'd looked at her with those marble eyes... she felt real.

And what she'd said to her.

What she'd told her.

You need to find me.

She remembered those words. And she remembered the place her and Keira were going now.

The North Lancs Barracks.

And somehow, she felt like that was exactly where she needed to go.

She took a deep breath of the cool, rainy air.

She swallowed a big lump in her throat.

And then she carried on walking down this road.

Empty inside.

Alone.

SARAH

* * *

"Keep still."

"I am keeping still."

"You're not keeping still. You're fidgeting."

"I'm doing my very best not to fidget."

"Well, try harder."

"Try harder not to fidget while a woman I barely know sticks a needle into my leg? Sure."

Carly rolled her eyes. "You're being dramatic."

If Sarah had never been accused of one thing in her life, it was being dramatic.

She'd been accused of the opposite quite a few times. Being inappropriately under-dramatic in situations where a little drama was expected. That was something of a speciality of hers.

In a way, she was grateful to hear someone accusing her of being dramatic. Perhaps she really was a changed woman after all. Perhaps her time with Nisha, Keira, and David really had transformed facets of her personality.

And she had to give the dog, Rufus, some credit too.

In a way, she rather missed them.

She sat in Carly's caravan. Dirty plates lay everywhere. The air was stuffy and sweaty. Flies buzzed against the blinds covering the windows, which were pulled right down.

And Carly was kneeling opposite her. Burying a needle into her ankle. Trying to stitch her up.

The pain made Sarah jolt, as much as she convinced herself she was remaining still. An XL Bully had bitten her. Which was infinitely preferable to being bit by an infected person, an admission she never imagined she'd make.

Her ankle burned and stung. Carly had doused it in alcohol, and now she was attempting to stitch it up with a needle that could *not* be sanitary, especially considering the conditions inside this caravan.

But beggars couldn't be choosers, could they?

And right now, she really was a beggar.

If she didn't get her leg stitched up, an open wound and all the potential for infection was a recipe for disaster.

Perhaps Carly's needle *would* infect her with something.

But it was a gamble she had to take.

So she held still. While Carly stitched her up. She looked focused. Concentrated. And to be honest, Sarah felt like she'd broken through a threshold of pain where it couldn't possibly get worse.

Carly applied a bandage around the wound. Then she sighed. Looked up at Sarah, glancing at her for just a moment.

"There," she said. "That should do the trick. For now."

Sarah nodded. *For now* was about as good as Sarah could expect.

She nodded back. "Thanks."

"Don't mention it," Carly said. "Drag you from the infected in the middle of a bridlepath. Come after you and stitch you up when you get yourself in trouble with those lunatics."

"I didn't ask for your help with them."

"Yeah, well, if I hadn't come to help you, you'd've been..."

She didn't continue. She stopped. Looked Sarah right in her eyes.

And Sarah knew why it was. Carly didn't want to admit it, but it was quite clear.

What Sarah had witnessed.

She was limping away from the campsite where those ruthless incel freaks had kidnapped her. She'd made them pay for what they'd put her through. Set their own dogs on them.

And walking away from them, listening to the leader's screams as his own dog tore him apart, she felt a sense of confidence she hadn't felt in years. A sense of *freedom* she hadn't felt all her life.

The freedom from her memories.

The freedom from her past.

The freedom from all the people who had used her.

All the people who had abused her.

Freedom.

But that freedom soon came crashing down when the infected approached her.

Surrounded her.

As she limped through the woods with her dog-bitten leg.

She stood there. Watched them circle her. Watched them hurtle towards her.

And she accepted her fate.

She accepted what was about to happen to her.

What was inevitable.

She stood there and waited, and then...

The infected.

They stopped.

They all just stopped.

Sarah stood there. Stared at them. She didn't understand. The only way it made sense was if Nisha was nearby.

But Nisha wasn't nearby.

And that's when she saw Carly.

And the bite mark on her arm.

And suddenly, it clicked. Even though it didn't make sense, it clicked.

Carly.

She was bitten.

She'd stopped the infected.

She was different in the same way Nisha was different.

And that opened up so many new possibilities.

But she didn't seem to want to talk about it. She seemed more focused on getting back here. On stitching Sarah up.

But neither of them had spoken about what happened next.

"What now?" Sarah asked.

Carly turned around. She put a pan over her portable stove and started heating something that smelled like soup. "You eat. You rest."

"And then what?"

Carly looked around at her as she stirred the pan, then looked away almost immediately. "I mean, what do you expect?"

"What you did out there—"

"I didn't do anything," Carly said.

"But that's not true. You *did*."

"I know what I did and didn't do. And I know what matters. It doesn't change anything. All that matters is I got back here. And you got back here, too."

"But the infected. You…"

"Look," Carly said, dropping the spoon in the pan and turning around, looking right at Sarah. "I came back for you. I helped you. And now we're here, and we survive here. Because that's how it is. That's how it has to be. It can't be any other way."

"But the bite. The infected. You… you're different."

"And there's nothing I can do about it but keep my head down and survive. Just like everyone else. And that's all you can do, too."

Sarah didn't quite understand Carly's motives. She understood her wanting to keep her head down. To survive.

But... *this?*

Was this all she wanted?

To hide away in this caravan? Especially with what she was capable of?

But then there was an irony to that, wasn't there?

And that irony was that... before the connections she'd built in recent weeks, Sarah would want exactly the same thing.

Carly was like a photo negative of Sarah.

And Sarah didn't like the old version of herself she was looking right at.

"I understand why you feel like you need to stay here," Sarah said. "But I told you. I have friends out there. Friends who need my help."

"And look where it got you last time."

Sarah remembered the group. Hanging from the trees. Their innards dangling from their bodies.

"Look," Carly said. "I... I get it. You want to find your friends. I get it. But if they're with... if they're with the group I think they're with. Then you have to believe me when I say..."

She stopped, then. Turned away again. Started stirring her soup even more vigorously.

"What?" Sarah asked. Standing. Which was a bad idea because her ankle was still in agony.

"Leave it," Carly said.

"I won't leave it. I'm not going to just leave it. Tell me what you know. The group they're with. This... *Leonard* you've spoken of. Who is he? And who are these people?"

She stopped again. She stared at the closed blinds. The caravan fell silent. The soup bubbled over the hob.

"Carly," Sarah said. "Speak to me. Please."

Carly stood there.

Unmoving.

Frozen.

She took a very audible deep breath.

And then she turned around to Sarah.

She opened her mouth like she was about to speak. Like she was about to tell her everything.

And then suddenly, out of nowhere, a bang.

At the caravan door.

Someone was here.

RICARDO

* * *

Ricardo looked out over the walls of his supposed "sanctuary" and tried to ignore the deafening screams from below.

It always happened around the same time every day. The experiments. The tests. Experiments he didn't want to think about. Tests he didn't want to think about. Some days, he saw the victims. Usually, people from the outside. Although there were more and more cases of people from within being used, now. Lawbreakers. Criminals. One day, you could be walking around this place without a care in the world. The next, you could be being used for the next great experiment. The next great test.

The screams echoed up from below. It sounded like a man. Begging. Crying out. In agony. In total agony.

Ricardo felt sick. He had an appetite earlier, but that appetite was gone now.

So he just stared out over the walls.

Stared out over the streets.

Stared off into the distance. And as dangerous as it was out there... he wished he could leave the confines of these walls.

He wished he could get away.

He saw burned-out buildings lining the street opposite. A message was laid across the roof of one of the terraced houses.

HELP US.

And in the early days of the infection, when Ricardo first started coming up here to watch the fireworks from within the safety of this place, he saw a figure at the window. He'd see movement. He'd hold up a torch, and he'd signal to them in patterns he didn't really understand. And occasionally, that person—man, woman, kid, he wasn't sure—would respond.

He never understood why that person hadn't attempted to cross the streets and reach this place. Maybe they heard the screams, too. Maybe they knew just from looking at it that this place was rotten to the very core.

Maybe they could see the decay from the outside, seeping through the barracks' dying veins.

He remembered the day he stopped seeing that figure. He was mildly worried about it the first time. But when the figure didn't appear for the second day and then the third day... he was actually rather sad.

Could he have done something to help?

Could he have gone out there and rescued whoever it was?

He knew that was strictly against protocol. Because the air was poisoned. That's why they had to wear their masks in here.

The air was poisoned. And the risks on the streets were too strong. No, they couldn't go out to help people.

People were welcome here. They were given an advanced screening at the gates, the details of which only the top brass truly understood—equipment provided by the government before the fall, apparently. Heat sensors. Shit like that.

Some made it through the gates. Some didn't.

But they had a community here.

A community of hundreds.

They had food here.

Not in abundance. But enough.

They had order here.

And until help arrived—help that Leonard continually insisted was on its way—they had enough.

But the narrative seemed to have shifted since the arrival of The Girl.

A sickly sensation filled his body when he thought about The Girl. Again, they were only whispers. But whispers travelled fast and lightly. And from what Ricardo had heard and so many others had heard, The Girl was different somehow.

She was special somehow.

She was resistant to the infection.

And she could do other things, too.

Things that Ricardo wasn't lucky enough to understand.

She was the key to the end of this nightmare.

That much Leonard was sure of.

He sat there. Looked over at the endless empty streets. At the abandoned cars. From this high vantage point—a place he liked to visit a lot—he saw figures drifting in this direction and in the opposite direction. There were a lot of people in the early days. But as the weeks passed ... the numbers of the infected grew, and the number of people slid.

It'd only been, what, a month?

And already, it felt like this wasn't man's world anymore.

It was the world of the infected.

He held on to his rifle. It felt alien in his hands. He hadn't had to use it much. Not inside, anyway. The rifles were more an intimidation device. More a sign of order. A reminder to anyone who might cause trouble of who was in charge.

And even though Ricardo didn't like to think of it that way... he had no doubt some of Leonard's goons wouldn't hesitate to wipe this place out if it meant securing their own survival.

Leonard's goons. Damn. Wasn't that *exactly* what he was?

He took a deep breath through the gas mask. The sweaty, slightly sour tang clawed across his lips. He wondered if it even made much of a difference. Apparently, it did. Apparently, when Ken Gruber ripped his mask off, he turned within minutes. Blood seeped from his eyes. He started spewing orange vomit all over the street.

They had to put him down.

For his own good.

For everyone's own good.

But as Ricardo sat there... he couldn't help wondering.

As safe as he was in here.

As abundant with supplies as this place was.

And as much as Leonard seemed hellbent on protecting this community...

Was this all there was?

Or was there more out there?

He heard another sharp, shrill cry. He squeezed his eyes shut and winced. His heart picked up. Raced.

He thought of Caroline.

Wherever she was.

Whoever she was with.

Despite everything... he still loved her.

He would always love her.

He listened to those screams, and he remembered Leonard's words.

"*We'll have to do some horrible things. Some unthinkable things. But everything is for the future. For our future. This nation will rise again. And it will start right here. At North Lancs.*"

He heard those words in his mind, and the screams intermingled with them. He looked down at the barren streets. He looked at that house with the *HELP US* sign laid across it.

And then he thought of the community here in the barracks.

He thought of the people he'd sworn to protect.

And of his friends.

He took a deep breath through the mask.

He tightened his grip around his rifle.

And then he stood up from the vantage point and walked away from the edge and back into the barracks.

Those agonised screams following his every step.

KEIRA

* * *

It was growing dark again, and Keira was no closer to the North Lancs barracks.

She was cold. Shivery. She couldn't see her breath in front of her, and Nisha wasn't wrapped up and didn't seem to be struggling either. So it must be her. A cold. Or the flu. Fuck. Just what she needed right now.

Then again, it was hardly surprising. The air reeked of shit. The drains were up. She hadn't been able to wash properly for weeks now. She'd grown used to that godawful feeling of clothes clinging to her skin with sweat. She stunk. She was sure of it. Everyone stunk.

She used to think watching celebrities in the jungle on that ITV show looked rough. She used to hate the thought of washing pots in the same water they swam in.

What she'd do for that luxury right now.

She walked down the dark road. She tried to walk as quietly as possible to avoid attracting the attention of any infected.

But more so, she could *hear* if any infected were nearby.

Or if *anyone* was nearby.

There were only two sets of ears between the three of them. And Keira wasn't entirely sure she wanted to delegate too much trust to Rufus, who grew just as excitable by the rustling of a squirrel as he did the infected.

She looked around at Nisha again. Walking along. Shoulders slumped. Quiet. Sure, she was always quiet. But she hadn't even written a thing in days.

And Keira felt... Well, she felt desperately sorry for this child. For this girl she was trying to protect. She wanted Nisha to feel like she could open up to her. It felt like they'd got some way along that road previously.

But as much as Keira wanted to deny it, she couldn't fool herself for very long.

Nisha had changed.

Something was going on inside Nisha.

She wanted to understand what it was.

She wanted her to open up to her.

But it just didn't seem like it was happening.

She took a deep breath of the cool night air. She was a little snotty. She realised then that her ears were ringing, her throat was sore, and her head was blocked. Shit. Just what she needed. Blocked sinuses to make hearing even more fucking difficult. Looked like Rufus was gonna have to pull his weight even more.

She walked further down this darkening road. She saw the sun glowing orange, setting. A shudder crept down her spine. Her stomach churned. They needed to find somewhere to rest for the night. They'd been walking for a solid three days now. They'd navigated their way around as many obstacles as possible—avoided main roads where they could, stuck to the fields. Any sign of life, and as instinctive as it might once have been for Keira to seek connection... she'd stayed away. Well away.

She'd been through a lot. A shitload. She'd lost Dad. She'd lost Sarah. She'd lost everyone.

But she hadn't lost Nisha.

She hadn't lost Rufus.

And she wasn't going to lose either of them.

She might be struggling. She might be finding this the most difficult test she'd ever encountered.

But she wasn't allowing fear or uncertainty or *anything* to define her anymore.

Reaching the North Lancs barracks with Nisha by her side.

That's all that mattered.

She walked another few steps when she noticed something.

Nisha.

She'd stopped.

She was standing in the middle of the road. Staring to her left. Into this old cafe. Betty's, apparently. It was all shuttered up. All boarded up.

And she was staring at it with wide eyes.

Keira let her stare for a few seconds. Even though her heart was racing. Even though it felt like darkness was intensifying. What was wrong with her? What was she looking at this place for? Was she having a turn again? God, Keira hoped not. She didn't know how she'd survived the last one. She was unconscious for a dangerous amount of time. And she hadn't even spoken about it since.

She wished Dad were here to give her answers.

To guide her.

She wished he was here to...

She took a deep breath.

Tightened her fists.

Dad wasn't here.

But she was still strong.

She always had been strong.

She put a hand on Nisha's shoulder.

Nisha looked up at her slowly. She didn't jump. She didn't flinch. She just looked up at Keira with this spaced-out gaze.

Keira thought about signing. One of the few fucking things she knew how to sign: you okay?

But instead, she reached into her rucksack.

She pulled out the notepad. Flipped over a few pages.

And then she sketched a few words down.

Nisha might not seem in the mood for talking.

But Keira was re-opening that line of communication. Whether she liked it or not.

She finished writing. Looked down at the words in front of her.

What's wrong? You see something?

She saw Nisha reading the words. She saw her focusing on them. Concentrating on them. Like she was struggling to read them. Struggling to understand them.

She saw her lift her pen.

Saw her press it to the paper.

She saw her begin to write something.

And then she looked up at the building again.

She stared at it with these wide eyes.

Peered at the cafe.

At the chairs stacked up outside.

Then, she pulled the pen away from the paper, and she handed the pad back to Keira.

She looked up at her.

Half-smiled at her. But it was very half-hearted. Not reassuring at all.

She shook her head in answer to Keira's question of whether something was wrong.

And then she began to walk again.

Keira wanted to stop her.

She wanted to ask her what the hell she was going to write.

She wanted to see inside her head.

Because as sorry as she felt for this kid... she had so many questions.

So many things she didn't understand.

She looked at Nisha as she slowly walked off down the road.

She looked back at the coffee shop.

She took a deep breath.

Then she patted Rufus' fur.

"Come on," she said. "Let's go find somewhere to shelter for the night."

She turned away from the coffee shop, and she walked after Nisha.

She couldn't shake the feeling that someone was lurking in the shadows of that old, abandoned coffee shop.

Watching.

SETH

*　*　*

Seth watched the woman, the girl, and the dog wandering down the street, and he couldn't even begin to explain how damned happy he was to see them.

Especially the lady.

Especially the lady.

He couldn't believe it at first. Couldn't believe it was actually her. She looked different. Everyone looked different. Of course, they did. Age did that. He looked different; he knew he did. Better? He wasn't sure.

But the lady...

He could still see the *girl* in her eyes.

The lady looked slim. Pretty. She had long dark hair, and she walked with a bit of a limp. The dog looked nice, too. A Labrador. One of his neighbours had a Labrador as a kid. His neighbour was called Theo. He used to take him dog walking sometimes. Mum always seemed happy to get Seth out of the way. She said he didn't get out enough. She always told him to go out on his bike and meet his friends.

But that showed how much she knew. 'Cause he didn't have any friends. He never had.

He wasn't sure what was wrong with him. But he was aware from a very young age that he was... different.

And it wasn't even in the way he dressed, the way he spoke, anything like that.

The other kids could just *smell* the difference in him.

They could see it from a mile away.

And that was something that hadn't changed for his entire damned life.

He wasn't sure whether that was because he'd distanced himself from other people. Through fear, mostly. Fear they might see him for who he was. Fear they might see how different he was. How *weird* he was.

But... he'd never know. He'd never made any friends. Mum was his best friend. His only friend.

And now she was...

He swallowed a lump in his throat. He took a deep breath of the warm, thick air. It smelled bad in here now. He didn't mind the smell so much at first. It reminded him of when he'd found a dead hedgehog by the side of the road when he was in his teens. The smell was so strong. It made his eyes water. It caught his attention so much that he turned his bike around and cycled past it just to find it.

He remembered finding it.

Remembered holding it in his palms.

And as he sat there on the side of the road, as the rain fell and the hedgehog lay still and cold in his hands... he felt a special kind of connection to it.

A special kind of *peace* in its presence.

He watched the lady, the girl, and the dog walk by, and he wondered whether this world could be different. He wondered whether he could make friends. Because they looked good people. They looked nice people.

And the lady. He *knew* she was a nice person. He'd known it when he was a child. And he knew it today.

She was what he had been waiting for all these years.

And if he couldn't make friends with them like this... well, they could join his mum.

And they could join his other new friends.

He stood up. Walked across the dirty plates lying on the living room floor. The old carpet was covered in cigarettes and patches of various liquids that'd been spilled over the years—wine, vomit, shit.

He reached the doorway into the dining room. The smell was so strong now. So intense. He stood there, and he closed his eyes, and he smiled. The smell used to disgust him. The smell used to make him sick.

But now?

It was the most beautiful smell Seth could imagine.

It made him feel special.

It made him feel at home.

He opened the door.

And when he saw his friends, he smiled.

When he saw Mum, he smiled.

When the smell surrounded him... he smiled even wider.

"Hello," he said, his voice raspy. Hoarse. "I've got some good news. I think I've found us some new friends."

He turned around.

Looked out of his front window.

Looked at the lady, the girl, the dog.

But mostly at the lady.

He smiled.

SARAH

* * *

Sarah heard the bang at the caravan door, and she froze.

Her heart started racing. Carly's eyes widened. She sat there in this dark, gloomy caravan, completely still. Her stitched-up ankle was still incredibly sore, incredibly tender. She really hoped she wouldn't have to get up any time soon. She really hoped there was a reasonable explanation for whoever was banging at the door. There had to be, didn't there?

But judging by the look on Carly's face, she was just as surprised as Sarah.

She was just as *scared* as Sarah.

Sarah sat there. Still. Very still.

Carly stood in front of her. Not moving. She didn't want to make a sound. Didn't want to make a single creak.

Whoever was here... she didn't want them to know they were here.

But there was only so long they could sit here and wait before...

Suddenly, a click.

The handle.

The handle of the caravan door.

Someone was trying to open it.

Someone was trying to get inside.

Sarah watched. The veins in her temples throbbing. She stared at that moving handle. Watched it shifting in slow motion. She saw Carly's face growing in redness. She could feel the air inside this caravan getting hotter. And her stomach felt like she was falling down the drop on a rollercoaster. A sensation she'd always despised.

She watched the handle inside the caravan shaking, shifting, until suddenly... it stopped.

It froze.

She sat there. The handle. Whoever was outside, they weren't trying to get in anymore.

The door.

It was locked.

But...

"The window," Carly said.

Sarah didn't know which window she was on about. The window opposite her was covered by an awful cream food-stained blind.

And then she saw the shadow move outside that window.

Behind that blind.

Suddenly, Carly reached across the caravan, over Sarah's shoulder, and yanked a blind down in front of a window that Sarah barely even realised was there. The window was caked in moss on the outside. Thick green moss.

But there were a few patches.

A few clear patches.

Carly pulled the blind down.

The blind came down.

But not in the way Carly hoped.

It tumbled off the sides of the window.

Snapped away.

Fell off.

And the movement made some of that moss fall off, too.

Exposing them.

Sarah stood there. Staring at the window. Heart racing. The blind. Collapsing. If someone thought the caravan was empty before... they wouldn't think so anymore.

And there was another problem.

Those footsteps.

Creeping around the side of the caravan.

Towards that window.

Carly looked at Sarah.

Sarah looked back at Carly.

There was only one thing both of them could do.

She ducked down.

Carly ducked down.

Both of them lay there on the small floor space of the caravan. A few flies buzzed around. Dust tickled Sarah's nostrils. Don't sneeze. Don't fucking sneeze...

She lay there on the floor. Heart racing. Shaking. Her leg aching. Those footsteps. Inching closer to that bare window.

She heard Carly muttering something under her breath. But it was hard to hear what she was saying.

And as that figure approached... Sarah wondered why Carly couldn't just stop them. If they were infected... she was pretty sure she'd seen what she'd seen already.

If they were infected.

That was the big *if* here.

What if they weren't infected?

What if they were someone else?

She lay there on the caravan floor when suddenly, she noticed a shadow at the window.

It was right there.

A figure.

Staring through a small crack in the moss.

She closed her eyes. Squeezed them shut.

She didn't want to see.

It felt like by closing her eyes, she was making herself less visible. She was more hidden.

But she knew that was just wishful thinking.

She was just as visible with her eyes closed as open.

But she lay there.

She squeezed her eyes shut.

She counted her breaths.

She was going to be okay.

Everything was going to be okay.

She had no idea how long she lay there on the caravan floor before finally opening her eyes.

The figure at the window was gone.

She looked up at the window for what felt like forever. She couldn't see any movement. She couldn't hear any movement, either.

Were they gone?

Had they given up?

She stayed there, lying there, heart racing. Regardless... she needed to get out of here. She needed to get away from here. She needed to find Keira, Nisha, and Rufus, too.

Because Carly... she'd just been on the verge of telling her the truth about this Leonard guy, whoever he was.

Some great secret.

And then they'd been interrupted by the bang at the door.

But whether she knew the truth or not, did it really change anything?

She needed to find Keira, Nisha, and Rufus.

One way or another, that was all that mattered.

She saw Carly looking up over her shoulder. Up towards the window. Then back at Sarah.

"They gone?" she asked.

Sarah looked at the window again. Then glanced back at Carly. "I wouldn't like to say."

They both waited a little longer before rising slowly. When they did, they looked out the window between the mossy cracks.

"Who the fuck was that?" Sarah asked.

Carly cleared her throat. "I don't... I don't know."

But Sarah didn't think she sounded entirely sure.

"Are you being honest with me?" Sarah asked as Carly wrestled with the blind and tried to put it up again.

"Help me get this back up," Carly said.

Sarah shook her head. "Why are you hiding so much?"

"Listen," Carly snapped. "There's things you don't understand. There's things you're better off not knowing about."

"About Leonard?"

"About everything," Carly shouted.

She looked at Sarah. Wide-eyed. And for the first time since Sarah met her... she thought she saw a look of fear in Carly's eyes.

"Look," Carly said. "I'll tell you what I can. But for now, we need to..."

She stopped.

Froze.

Stared up above Sarah.

Face paling.

Eyes widening.

"What?" Sarah said. "What is it?"

"Stay very still," Carly said.

Sarah frowned. Her heart started racing again. "What are you..."

"I said... stay very still."

Sarah wanted to stay still.

Every instinct in her body told her to stay still.

But she found herself turning.

Found herself looking up at where Carly was looking.

Right above her.

When Sarah saw what was staring down at her from the murky skylight, she wished she hadn't looked.

A man.

A grinning face.

Blood dripping from his cheeks.

Staining his sharp teeth.

And a bite mark.

Right across his neck.

"I said stay..."

She didn't hear what Carly said next.

Because that infected man pulled back his fist, smashed the skylight open, and dragged himself inside the caravan.

NISHA

* * *

Nisha hadn't heard the voice in her head for a long time. So when she heard it out of nowhere, in the middle of this dark, rainy road, it scared her.

It was really dark. Her and Keira were trying to find somewhere to stay for the night. But it had been night for a bit now, and they hadn't found anywhere. There weren't many houses where they were now. There were lots of fields on either side of them. Somewhere in the distance, she could see an old train on a track, totally still. There weren't many cars on this bit of road. And every time they walked past a car, she didn't want to look inside them.

She didn't want to see the blood.

She didn't want to smell the death.

They'd been walking forever. Her feet were sore. She hadn't eaten in a long time. She didn't really like eating anymore. Whenever she ate, she thought about herself in the bodies of the bad people. Chasing people. Hunting people. Biting people.

She thought of the man called Kevin. Back in the bunker.

She remembered how he tasted when she let the bad people get him, just to keep the voice happy.

And she didn't know how she'd done it. She didn't really understand why she had to do it, either. It just... made sense. Even though it *didn't* make any sense, it made sense to her deep down, like when Dad laughed and she knew she'd done something funny; she didn't know what, she just knew.

She hadn't heard the voice for a long time.

But that changed now.

You're taking us right where you need to, dear, right where we need to go, where we all need to go...

She didn't like the voice. It was hard to explain. Hard to explain how she could even *hear* it when she couldn't hear anything in the outside world. Maybe it was better to say she sort of *felt* it. Right in the middle of her chest.

But she guessed it was the voice of the bad people. And it was scary because it didn't sound *bad* like she *imagined* it to sound, even though she'd never heard anything before.

But there was something about how those words *felt* inside her chest that made her think that the voice didn't really care about her.

It only cared about itself.

But at the same time, in some way... there was something even scarier about that voice.

Something she didn't want to admit.

Something she didn't want to accept.

So she wasn't going to think about that right now.

She felt a hand on her back, and she jumped. She looked around. Saw Keira looking down at her.

You okay? she signed.

And Nisha felt bad for being annoyed at Keira for signing these same words. Because she was only trying to look after her. She was only trying to help her.

But there was a problem.

Every time she looked at Keira...

She saw Kevin's face.

She tasted the blood in her mouth.

And the worst thing?

A small part of her wanted to taste that blood again.

She nodded. Then she looked over at Rufus. He was staring at her. The hairs on his back raised tall again. He looked at her for a few seconds, and then his eyes moved slightly to the side. Like he didn't want to look her in the eyes.

And it made Nisha sad. Because Rufus was nice before, but it was like he *knew* there was something different about her.

Like he *knew* something was wrong with her.

Like he *knew* something was changing.

Deep inside her.

She felt Keira's hand on her shoulder again. She looked around and saw the piece of paper in front of her. The notepad.

Won't walk much further tonight. Get sleep soon.

And again, Nisha felt bad. Because Keira was trying her best. But it was so hard to explain to her. She wouldn't understand.

She wouldn't understand what was going on inside Nisha.

She wouldn't understand the voice.

She wouldn't understand what it was making her do.

And she never will understand.

She can never know.

You just need to keep walking...

She hadn't seen The Girl for a long time. That scared her. She didn't even know if The Girl was real. But it *felt* like she was real.

But she hadn't seen her in a long time. She hadn't seen her in her dreams.

Was she okay?

And if she wasn't... what did it mean?

And...

What if she *was* just in her head, like a dream? Dad always said she got over-excited about her dreams.

What if this girl was just a way of her trying to feel like she hadn't lost everyone?

She had an imaginary friend when she was younger. She was called Fox. She was sometimes a person with red hair and sometimes a fox. She liked doing everything with Fox. And Fox could *speak*, and Nisha could understand her.

Sometimes, Dad tried to tell her Fox wasn't real. She was an imaginary friend. But that upset Nisha. Especially since it upset Fox, too.

In her dreams, she heard Fox speak. She heard her talk. And she understood her.

And there was a part of Fox's voice that reminded her of...

Of the voice.

I'm still here I'm still with you I'll always be with you...

She stood there in the darkness.

She looked up at Keira.

And as silly as she thought her signing and writing in the notebook was... she took the pen and paper and then wrote.

Thank you. Hope you're okay.

She handed the notepad back to Keira.

Watched her read the words.

She saw her eyes well up and go all red.

Then she looked down at Nisha, and she smiled at her, but she looked sad.

She held a hand to her heart.

Nodded.

Thank you, too.

Nisha looked at Keira as they stood there in the rainy darkness.

She looked at Rufus, who cowered away. Whose hairs stood on his back. Who looked like he was growling.

She wasn't a bad person.

Even though she felt different, even though she felt like she was changing... she wasn't a bad person.

She was going to be okay.

Everything was going to be okay.

She felt a hand wrap around her back and hold her close.

Keira.

Hugging her.

Tight.

And as she held her close... she couldn't get rid of the voices in her head.

Scratching in her mind.

We're coming, dear, we're close, we're following, we're with you all the way, we're with you every step of the way...

And Nisha thought about the thing she didn't like to admit about that voice.

That voice wasn't Fox's.

That voice was hers.

You are Mother.

And we're coming for you.

We're coming home to you.

LEONARD

* * *

Leonard believed in the idea that if you exposed yourself to something enough, you could grow accustomed to even the worst horrors imaginable.

But seeing the gory, violent scene in front of him, the way it made his stomach turn, he wasn't sure how true that was.

The floor of the old garage area was covered in blood and innards. Intestines wormed around the floor like the shed skin of snakes. There was a real raw, meaty smell to the air. Like the butcher on the market he used to have to walk past whenever he was doing charity work for the military in the city centre.

One of the worst smells in the world.

And he'd smelled some seriously bad smells.

He'd smelled stacks upon stacks of dead bodies in the Middle East.

He'd smelled a human body, burned alive.

But there was something primal about that raw meat smell. Something that broke through to his very core.

And there was also something exciting about it.

Something *powerful* about it.

Because of its potential.

He looked at The Girl. She was sitting across the room. Chained up. She looked pale. Tired. Her nosebleeds were getting worse. She was bleeding from her ears now, too. It looked like she was crying.

And it was a lot to put The Girl through. Everyone kept telling him that.

But everyone that kept telling him that didn't understand. They couldn't. Not truly.

Because this girl was special.

This girl was the key.

She was the answer.

To everything.

He held his rifle. Looked at the infected man yanking against his chains. And at the bitten, torn remains of the man on the ground. He was from the inside. Caught stealing some food. Rations he wasn't entitled to.

And sure, it might appear a harsh punishment. It may seem a little excessive in the grand scheme of things.

But the way Leonard saw it... he wasn't just a military leader anymore.

He was a scientist.

And he was pioneering the greatest, most powerful discovery potentially of this nation's history.

Of this world's history.

He walked over towards The Girl, being careful to keep a close eye on the man lying on the ground, chained at the ankles to stop him from straying too far. He'd seen what she'd done. What she was capable of. She'd been bitten. Only she hadn't changed, like everyone else. And at the time, that seemed like a momentous discovery in itself.

But it went beyond that.

Far, far beyond that.

She could repel the infected.

She could hold them back.

And as their studies continued... it became clear that she could exert some kind of *control* over them, too.

But even *that* wasn't the most exciting discovery.

The most exciting discovery?

He'd had a taste of it.

They'd all had a taste of it.

It felt like they were ninety per cent there. Like they were so, so close to the possibility.

He'd seen what she could do.

He'd got glimpses of what she could do. Of what she was capable of.

And still, he felt like he was barely scratching the surface.

He reached The Girl. Crouched down. Held her cold, shaking hands.

"It's okay, my love," he said. "It's me."

She shuddered a little. Her teeth chattered together.

"When can I see him again?" The Girl asked. Which was kind of sweet. For a blind girl.

He thought about The Girl's dad.

The way he'd fought so selflessly to get her here.

But how he wouldn't stop fighting.

How he just wouldn't shut up...

And at the end of the day, he was being selfish. Because this girl. Sure, she might be that man's daughter. But she was more than that. Way, way more.

She was potentially their way out of the grips of this infection.

Or even better.

She was potentially the key to *controlling* this infection.

And whoever controlled the infection controlled it all...

So he'd had to deal with her father.

In the most humane way possible.

A bullet to the back of the head when he wasn't looking.

Wouldn't've known a thing about it.

He felt bad about it. He was having to use his own people for the experiments at this point. What he'd do for an influx of new arrivals. What he'd give for that.

Because using his own people. Even though he *knew* it was for the greater good... it still felt so wrong.

"Soon," Leonard said. Squeezing her hands a little tighter. "You can see him very, very soon. Not many more experiments to go now. You just have to keep doing what I tell you. You just have to make sure you don't misbehave. And you just need to make sure you don't do anything silly, and everything will be okay. Understand?"

She appeared to look right at him with those dead, vacant, empty eyes.

He nodded back at her. Started to stand. "Have you seen *her* again?"

The Girl was silent. She didn't say a thing.

"Because... if what you say about her is true. She's important. Finding her. Bringing her here. That's... the most important thing of all. Isn't it?"

She looked at him with those empty eyes. And for a second, for just a second, it felt like she was looking right at him.

Like she could see.

And honestly, it scared him to death.

"Anyway," he said. "I'll be back. For more experiments. And then... we can think about letting you see Dad, can't we?"

He smiled at her.

She didn't smile back.

Leonard gulped.

He turned around.

He jumped.

The infected—the one that'd just been torn to pieces—was on its feet.

Blocking his path.

Standing right in front of him.

He saw it standing there.

Staring at him.

Almost like it was staring right *through* him.

And for a moment, for just a moment... he felt fear.

He felt... afraid.

And then the infected staggered to the left.

Stumbled back down to the floor.

Leonard hurried past it.

He looked back at The Girl.

Looked at her, sitting there in the darkness, chained up.

Staring right at him.

For a moment, he swore she was looking at him right in the eyes.

And for a moment, thinking about that infected man, writhing around on the floor, chained at the ankles... he wondered whether he was insane for seeing it how he'd seen it, for just a moment.

A threat.

A sign that The Girl was getting stronger.

A sign that the balance of power was shifting.

That a storm was on the horizon.

And it was getting closer and closer...

SARAH

* * *

The infected man smashed his fists against the glass rooftop hatch and clambered inside the caravan.

Glass rained down on Sarah's face from above. She felt a few sharp shards nicking her cheeks. The infected man crawled inside the caravan, mouth wide, blood spilling from his lips. The caravan. It wasn't safe anymore. They weren't safe in here.

"Out the way!" Carly shouted. "Quick!"

Sarah didn't even have time to think about it. She just staggered back, away from the tumbling infected man, as he fell into the caravan.

He landed right in front of Sarah. Slammed against the floor. Made the caravan shake.

His neck snapped up, and then he looked at Sarah with these dead eyes.

This demonic smile across his face as blood oozed down his chin on that cramped floor space. Barely enough floorspace for her and Carly to fit on, let alone an infected lunatic.

A hand grabbed her back. She jumped a little. Another infected? Inside the caravan?

But it was Carly.

Looking at the infected man with wide eyes.

She dragged Sarah out of the way.

Stepped in front of her.

Squared up to the infected man.

And it seemed like madness. It seemed like lunacy. She couldn't do this. She couldn't endanger herself like this.

But then… she'd seen what Carly could do. She'd seen what Carly was capable of. She was going to hold her back. Just like Nisha could.

The infected man scrambled to his feet.

And then he rushed towards Carly.

He tackled her to the caravan floor.

Sent her tumbling back.

Smacking her head against the floor.

And as Sarah stood there, as she watched the infected man's mouth inch towards Carly's throat… a sickening realisation sunk in.

This infected man.

He wasn't like the others.

For whatever reason… Carly couldn't hold him back.

Which meant she was in danger.

She was in big danger.

His teeth inched towards her throat.

And even though she'd shown previous resistance to the infection, judging by the bite mark on her arm… a bite to the neck was bad news for anyone.

She needed to do something.

She needed to help her.

She looked around this kitchen area. She looked at the kitchen worktop. Saw plates stacked up by the sink. Saw cutlery lying on the units.

But nothing heavy.

Nothing sharp.

And there was no time to fuck around.

She looked down at the infected man.

Pinning Carly down by her arms.

And...

There was something different about Carly.

Her eyes.

Rolled back into her head.

Blood streaming from her eyelids.

She was trying something.

She was trying. But she was failing.

She knew there was no more time.

She knew there was nothing else she could try.

She pulled back her foot and booted the infected man in the forehead.

Hard.

The man's head snapped back. And even though it wasn't much, it gave her enough time to think. It bought Carly some time, too.

But that clock was ticking.

Time was running out.

She pulled back her foot again and went to kick again.

And then she heard something that made her freeze.

Banging.

At the door.

And shrieking.

More infected. More fucking infected.

Outside.

One right here on the caravan floor.

And one outside.

Banging at the door.

Or *more* than one.

Fuck. She didn't know. She had no fucking idea.

But it didn't really matter if this one bastard in here tore them both apart.

She pulled back her foot again. Went to kick this bastard in the head. Outside, the infected banged at the door. Fingernails scratched at the door.

And the caravan rattled and shook as they threatened to overwhelm the place.

And then she saw something.

On the floor. Right beside the infected man.

A shard of glass.

A sharp shard of glass.

Sharp enough to use on the infected man.

If only she could reach it...

She looked down at the piece of glass right there beside the infected man.

Right beside Carly.

And that infected man.

Teeth snapping.

Inching towards Carly.

And so close to that piece of glass.

The banging at the door.

The open skylight above.

And this infected man and Carly, on the floor right in front of her.

She couldn't just leave Carly.

She had to help her.

After everything Carly had done for her... she couldn't just leave her.

She reached down, and she grabbed the shard of glass and—

The infected man's head darted towards her fingers.

She felt his damp teeth scraping against the outside of her fingers.

She yanked her hand away.

Just in time.

She stamped on the bastard's neck.

And then she buried the shard of glass deep into the bastard's throat.

She yanked it to the side. Dragged it. Dragged it as more blood pooled out.

She pulled it out then, and then she slammed it into his temple.

Cracked the bone.

Pushed it in deeper, as blood splattered up onto her hands.

She kept on pushing that shard of glass down as she pressed her foot on his shaking, twisting neck.

She kept on standing on his throat as she buried that shard of glass deeper and deeper into his skull.

She kept her foot there as she held the piece of glass there and...

And suddenly, the infected man gasped.

Suddenly, his eyes closed.

The blood drained out.

And he was still.

She kept her foot there for a few seconds, shaking on his neck. She wanted to make sure he wouldn't just spark back to life.

She looked at Carly. Saw her eyes were open now. Looking around as the blood trickled from her eyes.

"Come on," Sarah said, holding out a hand. "We need to get away from here."

"It didn't... I couldn't..."

A bang at the door.

Even harder.

And smacking at that window, too. The one behind the blind.

"We can talk when we're out of here," Sarah said. "But right now... we really need to go."

She reached down.

She grabbed Carly's hand.

She pulled her to her feet.

"Come on," Sarah said, looking up at the skylight. "We have to..."

No sooner had she spoken that she noticed something.

Two things.

The door.

The caravan door.

It bashed open.

And the caravan filled with cool air and shrieks.

And then... something else, too.

Another infected.

A woman this time.

Lying on the top of the caravan.

Dragging herself towards the skylight.

They were trapped.

They were surrounded.

There was no way out.

KEIRA

* * *

They found an old farmhouse up the road and decided to stay there for the rest of the night, even though most of the night had already passed.

Keira couldn't sleep even though she was exhausted. She sat by the door and stared out into the darkness. Nisha was lying on the sofa. They'd scanned the place when they got here. Spent a good while going around every room, making sure it was empty. A nervous search.

But it was okay. Everything was quiet. Everything was fine. Nobody was home. And it didn't look like anyone had lived here in quite a while.

It was a really old place. There was a caravan in the garden and some scaffolding on the side of the house. Looked like maybe someone was beginning to renovate this place before the infection struck. Clearly hadn't got very far. The place was filled with dust. Old furniture. Creepy old family photos that looked ancient.

But it would do as a shelter. If anything, the creepiness of the place would keep any dodgy people away.

As for the infected... well, she wasn't sure the creepiness of a place was such a deterrent.

She stroked Rufus. He lay on the floor, sighing like he'd had the most stressful day of all. She'd fed him a few scraps. Eaten a few scraps herself. Offered Nisha some, but she just picked at it. She thought back to the incident on the road. The cafe. Nisha, standing there, staring inside it. Looking through those darkened windows like there was something there.

Some*one* there.

She'd given up trying to communicate with Nisha. At the end of the day, for whatever reason, Nisha didn't seem comfortable communicating with Keira anymore. So her primary focus was getting this kid to the North Lancs barracks. Seeing what was there. Finding out about this "antidote" talk.

And hopefully, finding somewhere safe enough to look after Nisha.

To protect her.

To keep her safe.

That was her duty. That was her goal.

And it was all she truly cared about.

She looked around at the sofa, half-expecting to see Nisha lying there when she saw her standing right behind her.

There was something undeniably creepy about Nisha, standing there in the dark, silently staring out the window. Especially since she looked so pale. Especially the way her long hair dangled down the front of her body. Kind of reminded her of something out of The Grudge or one of those other Eastern horror movies in the 2000s.

She felt immediately guilty for feeling that way. Nisha was just a child. She'd lost a lot. She'd lost so much.

But she couldn't shake the feeling that something was changing inside her.

And it was making Keira more uncomfortable.

But then Nisha walked towards her. She sat down right beside her. Rufus got up right away. Walked across the room to the other side. Sat down, curled in a ball. Stared right at Nisha. He didn't want to be anywhere near her. He sensed the change, too.

Keira was tempted to try to communicate with her. To ask her what was going on inside her. Because something was. And she wanted to know what. She *needed* to know what.

But she didn't want to pressure the girl. She'd pressured her enough.

So she sat there. Stared into the darkness. It wasn't sleep. But it was rest. And in this world, when you spent most waking hours filled with adrenaline... it was enough.

And then Nisha nudged her.

She looked around.

Nisha was holding the notepad. She handed it to her. And there was writing on there. Hard to make out in the dim light of night. But undeniable.

She looked up at Nisha. Looked down at the notepad, there in her hands.

She squinted at the words staring up at her.

I want to talk but it might scare you.

A shiver crept down Keira's spine. Here it was. An opportunity. An opportunity for Nisha to open up. And an opportunity for Keira to learn the truth about what was going on inside her head, too.

She took the pen, and she wrote back: *If you want to talk about anything, I'm here for you.*

Nisha took the pad back from Keira. Waited a few seconds. Then wrote again.

At first, the bad people stopped, and I didn't know how, but now I can see through their eyes and stop them. Or make them do things, too.

She read those words, and a lump swelled in Keira's throat.

So there it was.

Confirmation.

Confirmation that Nisha was even stronger, even more powerful than first realised.

But Nisha hadn't stopped writing there.

I feel tired now, though, like I can't stop them anymore.

That wasn't good. That wasn't good at all.

There's something else too.

Keira looked at her. Sitting there. Holding the pad. Holding the pen.

She smiled at her. Nodded. She wanted to show her it was okay. It was okay to open up. It was okay to be honest.

Nisha looked down at the pad.

She started to write.

And suddenly... from deep inside the confines of the house, Keira heard something that sent a shiver crawling right up her spine.

A voice.

A high voice.

"Please don't hurt me. Please don't hurt me. Please..."

SARAH

* * *

Sarah heard the infected banging down the caravan door.

She saw the infected woman dragging herself towards the skylight.

And even though she'd buried a knife into the temple of the infected man on the floor... he was still twitching.

They were trapped.

Her and Carly were trapped inside this caravan.

And there was no way out.

The windows smashed open.

The one on the left.

And then the one on the right.

The infected woman dangled down from above. Shouting. She sounded like she was speaking in tongues. And it sent shivers down Sarah's spine.

All she could do was stand there on the caravan floor.

Carly by her side.

Staring at the infected racing inside with tears of blood trickling down her cheeks.

For whatever reason, Carly's resistance wasn't working anymore.

Her shield... it wasn't working.

Sarah grabbed her. Because it was the only thing she could do.

"The back of the caravan."

"But the window's stuck—"

"I don't care whether the window's stuck or not. The back of the caravan. Now."

She dragged Carly through the main area of the caravan.

Staggered towards the door right at the back, as much as her wounded leg would allow.

The woman tumbled down through the skylight and hit the floor with a thump.

And another man fell with her, too.

Landed right by her side with a thud.

She ran to the door. Grabbed it with her shaking hand. Opened it. Swung the door open.

And then, as the infected approached... she slammed it shut.

A hand stuck between the crack in the door, blocking her from closing it properly.

She pushed against it.

Hard.

So hard she heard a crack in the bone.

She gritted her teeth.

Pulled it back again.

Then, slammed it harder, and...

The door.

Cracking the arm.

She pushed against it. Carly rushed to the side of the bed. Climbed on it, started trying to unlock the window. "It won't budge!"

"Try smashing it," Sarah said.

Carly shook her head. Looked around. "I don't have anything to..."

"Use your fucking imagination," Sarah said as she pressed against that door.

She held back the mass weight of the infected, banging at the door.

She held it as she heard the flimsy wood breaking.

Snapping.

Cracking.

She watched Carly bang and bang and kick the window.

"It's—it's not breaking," she said. "It's just not..."

Suddenly, the window cracked.

Split into pieces.

And Sarah sensed an opportunity.

Sarah sensed a chance.

An opportunity to run.

A chance to get away from here.

To get out of here.

"Quick," Sarah said. "Now!"

Carly looked around the bedroom. Wide-eyed.

And then she climbed out, over the glass, outside.

The infected banged at the door behind Sarah.

She stood there, holding back that force, and she knew she needed to go for it.

She knew she needed to run.

She knew time was running out.

She gritted her teeth.

She held her breath.

"Now or never," she said. "Now or fucking—"

The door split.

The infected cracked through.

Hands.

Grabbing her.

Pulling her back.

She yanked against them. Dragged herself away. She stumbled

across the bedroom and towards that open window that Carly had just tumbled out of.

"Come on," she muttered as the infected raced after her. "Come on…"

She climbed towards the window. She felt the glass nick against her palm as she tried to drag herself out and felt the cool air from outside hit her face.

She dragged herself over that window. She couldn't see Carly anywhere. But that was probably a good thing. Because there were infected on her left. Turning around. Growling at her. Close. So close.

She dragged herself out of that window when suddenly, she felt a hand on her dog-bitten ankle.

Squeezing against it.

Squeezing so hard it made her yelp.

She kicked out.

She flailed around.

She tried to break free of that tightening grip.

But she couldn't.

She just couldn't.

It was too tight.

Holding her too hard.

There was no way out.

There was no getting away.

She gritted her teeth as the pain wracked through her body when suddenly, she saw Carly appear.

She saw her swing something right over her shoulder.

A blade.

Some kind of machete.

It was so close to her. So close it almost cut her own leg off in the process.

But her leg was free.

Carly grabbed her hands. "Quick. Come on."

She pulled her out of the window.

She dragged her out, and she hit the ground with a thump.

Carly dragged her back up. "We've got to go. Now."

Sarah clambered up to her feet as pain wracked her body.

She looked over her shoulder at the infected, dragging themselves out of the caravan window.

She looked at the infected emerging around the side of the caravan.

Racing after them both.

And she saw the caravan itself.

This place of temporary security.

This place of temporary shelter.

Gone.

Carly squeezed her hand. And when Sarah looked at her, she swore she saw tears streaming down her face.

"Now," she said. "Run."

And then, as much pain as Sarah was in, as sore as her leg was, and as exhausted and as broken as she felt... she didn't have a choice.

She turned around from the approaching infected.

Carly's hand in hers.

And then, together, both of them ran.

KEIRA

* * *

Keira heard the terrified scream from somewhere in the house.

It was only once. And that made her wonder if she was imagining it. She'd barely slept in weeks, so a hallucination wasn't exactly abnormal. Yesterday, she swore someone stepped right up to her and blew a puff of air in her face within the space of a blink. Yeah. Exhaustion-induced hallucinations were just another shitty part of this incredibly shitty new world.

But something told her this wasn't a hallucination.

Something told her this was real.

She turned around. Looked across the lounge. Saw Rufus, by the door, growling. Staring out into the hallway. Fuck. He'd heard something, too. Which meant it wasn't in her head.

She wasn't hallucinating. That was the good news.

The bad news?

There was someone in the house.

Her heart raced faster. The living room shadows surrounded

her. That voice. A child's voice. Begging for help. Begging someone not to hurt them.

Infected?

The infected could mimic the uninfected. She'd come across it a couple of times now. It seemed pretty primitive. But it was another fucking terrifying possibility to have to contend with. Something she could do without. Something they could all do without.

She felt Nisha's hand squeeze hers.

She looked around.

Saw Nisha staring at her. Almost like she wanted to know what the hell was going on. What the hell had caught her attention.

Keira gulped. *It's okay*, she signed.

She turned around, then, to the living room door. She grabbed a cricket bat wrapped in barbed wire she'd put together to defend herself, Nisha, and Rufus if she needed to. Stood there, heart racing. They were okay in here. They were safe in here. If they needed to get out, they could break through the living room window and escape that way. There was nothing to be gained from trying to find the source of the voice. There was nothing at all to be gained from searching for it. There was...

"Help!"

A yelp.

A desperate, pained yelp.

And it was coming from...

The kitchen?

Fuck. She couldn't just stay in here listening to that voice all night. She needed to go outside this room. And she needed to investigate.

But at the same time... she didn't want Nisha coming to any danger.

She looked around at Nisha. She could get in their heads. She could control them. Make them do things. Or stop them doing things.

But right now, she didn't look like she usually looked when the infected were close.

Right now, she looked... confused.

She didn't look like she'd looked the last few days. Almost like that creepy, cold exterior had cracked a little.

Right now, she looked like the child she was when Keira first met her.

Vulnerable.

Afraid.

Keira grabbed the notepad. She turned the page.

Stay right here, she wrote. *I'll be right back.*

She handed it to Nisha.

Nisha read the words. Studied them closely.

And then she wrote something back to her.

Handed the notepad back to her.

Please be okay.

Keira swallowed a lump in her throat.

She looked back at Nisha, and she nodded. Smiled. Choking back the tears.

After all these days of disconnect and serious concern for where Nisha was at—and for what was happening to her internally—it felt like they were close again.

She turned around and walked past Rufus towards the door.

She opened the door. Slowly. Went to close it with Rufus and Nisha in there.

But Rufus wasn't having it.

He scratched the door.

Panted.

Turned around to look at Nisha with fear in his eyes, then back at Keira.

And... and as much as Nisha just broke through that undeniable air of creepiness that'd surrounded her lately, Keira still felt uncomfortable leaving Rufus alone with her when he was this terrified.

"Come on," she muttered, pushing the door open just enough so he could get through. "But stay close. I don't want anything happening to you. Okay?"

He nudged her leg. Wagged his tail. Clearly just relieved to get out of the room Nisha was in.

Keira looked over at Nisha, standing by the window, her silhouette illuminated by the glow of the moonlight. Staring back at her with those wide eyes.

"You'll be okay," she whispered. Mostly to herself.

And then she closed the living room door and turned around to face the hallway's darkness.

She stood there. Shaking. Heart racing. Staring down the long, dark hallway corridor. That voice. She swore it'd come from the kitchen.

But the kitchen door was open. And as far as she could tell, there was nobody in there.

She stood in the corridor, heart racing, knees quivering. She was making a mistake. She needed to stay in that living room with Nisha. Guard it. Stand in there and guard it and prepare her escape route, just in case.

She went to turn back around when she heard the voice again.

"Please... help me... please..."

She stood there. A cold shiver spread down her spine and arms.

That voice.

It wasn't coming from the kitchen.

It was coming from the cupboard under the stairs.

She walked towards it.

Slowly.

Holding the barbed-wire cricket bat in hand.

She reached the door.

Heart racing.

What was she doing?

She needed to stay away.

She needed to go back to the living room.

She was safer there.

Nisha was there.

"Please. Help. Anyone. Please..."

She swallowed a lump in her throat.

Looked down at Rufus, who pawed the door to the cupboard under the stairs.

She lifted her machete.

Reached for the handle.

Lowered it.

She held her breath.

Braced herself.

Here goes nothing...

And then she opened the door.

Much to her relief, an infected person didn't come lunging out at her.

But there was something in the darkness of that cupboard under the stairs that did surprise her.

Steps.

Dusty old steps, leading down into a cold, dark cellar.

She stood there. Shaking. Staring into the dark. This was madness. This was craziness. This was—

"Please!"

That whimpering voice.

Down in the cellar.

What if it *wasn't* an infected?

What if someone genuinely needed help?

She stood there. Looked around at Rufus, who whined. Whimpered.

Then she looked back at the darkness.

She held the machete close.

She took a deep breath.

And then she walked through the door.

She stood at the top of the steps.

Heart racing.

Skin on fire.

She looked down into the darkness below.

She gulped.

She closed her burning eyes.

This is madness.

This is craziness.

But you can't just leave them down there.

She took another deep breath.

And then, without thinking about it for another second, she climbed down the stairs.

One step at a time.

Every step echoing as she got further and further down.

She walked further, Rufus right beside her. The darkness engulfed her even more.

But she could see something down in the darkness.

Right at the bottom.

Light.

Flickering light.

She walked. Even though this felt crazy, she walked.

She kept on walking and walking until she reached the bottom step.

She stood there.

The candlelight flickering, illuminating the wall.

And the shuffling figure right around the side of that wall beside her.

Infected?

Or someone in need of help?

She was about to find out.

She gritted her teeth.

Looked back up the steps.

Nisha. She hoped she was okay. She should be with her right now. Shouldn't leave her.

She tightened her fists.

She took another deep breath.

And then she stepped around the wall and stared towards the flickering light and the source of the scream.

When she saw what was sitting there, Keira couldn't quite process it.

She couldn't quite understand it.

But one thing was for sure.

Whoever this was, they weren't infected.

It was far, far scarier than that.

NISHA
---

* * *

Nisha looked through the window and thought someone was standing in the darkness.

It was really dark outside. She could see the moon before and liked it when she could see the moon. It reminded her of when she was tucked up in bed at home. Awake in the middle of the night. If she saw the light peeking through the curtains, she would open them and stare at the moon as it shone down on her.

She'd lie there for what felt like forever. She'd stare out of the window and up at the moon. And even if she didn't get back to sleep again that night, it didn't matter 'cause the glow of the moon made her feel like she was getting all the rest she needed.

She couldn't see the moon right now. Only the dark clouds in the sky.

And that movement. Somewhere in the distance.

Creeping closer.

She stood there by the lounge window. She didn't know where Keira had gone. But she looked worried. Which meant she must've heard something, and now she was going to check it out.

But it was weird because Nisha didn't feel scared anymore. She didn't feel afraid of what Keira might find. She couldn't *feel* the bad people close to her. So... that was a good thing, wasn't it?

She looked through the window, out into the dark.

She stared out into that dark, and she buried her fingernails into her hands, and she felt herself...

Searching.

Searching for *something*.

Squeezing her fingers deep into her palms and staring out into the dark and—

The Girl.

Only she was... somewhere different.

She was in a different room.

A darker room.

And her eyes didn't look like marbles anymore.

They looked right at her.

Deep into Nisha's eyes.

And she wanted to speak to her. She wanted to open her mouth, and she wanted to speak to her, but...

She felt so far away.

So, so far away.

Nisha concentrated harder. She clenched her teeth like she did when trying to force herself to hear. She tasted blood in her mouth as the image of The Girl grew clearer and clearer in her mind.

And then she could...

Hear something.

Those tingles.

Those tingles on either side of her head.

Whispers.

She strained harder. She still couldn't hear properly. Or maybe she *could* hear properly, but she just couldn't understand the words. Because why *would* she understand the words? She'd never heard in her life, other than in the dreams.

So why would she suddenly be able to understand those words in her dreams now?

But she clenched her teeth harder. She focused harder.

She focused so hard that she tasted the blood in her mouth, even stronger, and felt its warmth trickling down onto her lips and down her chin...

And suddenly, she was trapped in this place.

Trapped in this dark place, and she couldn't get out of it.

Because the hands were squeezing her body and throat.

And the little sharp teeth were biting her arms.

And the *bats*—

All flying past her.

All screeching.

All—

She opened her eyes and gasped.

She was back in the room again. Back in the dark again. The moon was still hiding behind the clouds. She could taste blood on her lips. When she reached up and wiped her face, she felt something damp on her fingers. When she looked at her hand, she saw blood.

She stood there. Heart racing. She turned around to the door Keira had disappeared through. She felt this sudden urge to get to her. Close to her. Because... she couldn't explain why, but it felt like something was wrong. Something was very wrong.

She walked across the room towards the door when suddenly she felt this burning pain in her head. Splitting, cracking, right behind her eyes.

She froze. She curled over. Clutched her stomach and lower chest.

The taste of blood. Getting even stronger in her mouth.

And that pain in her head, right through her body, getting stronger and stronger, and...

Suddenly she *FELT* it.

Those words.

Right in the depths of her chest.

We're coming for you we're following we're coming and we'll be there you're leading us there and everything will be okay everything will be...

But these words. They didn't make any sense to her.

None of it made any sense to her.

She could only stand there clutching her stomach.

She could only stand there, trying to breathe, trying not to vomit.

She could only stand there and...

A flash.

An image.

Bright in her mind.

An image of a body.

Only it wasn't like a body she'd seen before.

It was like a *snake's* body.

Only...

This snake was huge.

This snake was stretching across fields, streets, and towns.

And then, when the image in her head grew clearer... suddenly, Nisha realised it wasn't a snake at all.

It wasn't a body at all.

It was...

She opened her eyes again.

She stood up. Shaking. Sweating. Heart racing really fast in her chest in that way it always did, in that way that made her feel so dizzy.

She needed to find Keira.

She needed to warn Keira.

'Cause she'd seen something.

She'd seen something in her head, and even though it might not be real, even though it might all be in her mind...

It *felt* real.

And she needed to tell her about it.

She went to run towards the door when suddenly, she got the feeling she was being watched.

She stopped.

Stood there in the darkness.

Stood there in this dusty, empty living room.

And then she turned around.

Slowly.

Outside the window, she saw figures.

Standing there.

Staring in through the glass at her.

And then, all of them, running towards her.

KEIRA

* * *

Keira had seen some pretty horrible sights in the month since the virus broke out and spread across the nation. She'd seen unforgettable sights. Things she'd never etch from her memory.

She'd seen violence.

She'd seen trauma.

And she'd seen so much death.

But in terms of twisted, in terms of fucked-up... very few things matched up with the sight in front of her right now.

She stood at the foot of the cellar stairs. The cellar was poorly lit. It smelled damp and dusty. Mould crept across the old brick walls. There was a dampness to the floor, too. Really felt like nobody had been down here for a long, long time.

But there was someone sitting there in the middle of the room.

In the slightest, faintest glow of the candle.

A man.

He was sitting on a wooden stool. His ankles were tied to the legs of the stool. His hands were tied behind his back. He was naked. And there was a rope tied around his throat. It was so tight that it looked like it was keeping him firmly in place. Stopping him from budging anywhere at all.

Even though it was dark, Keira could see the sweat and the blood dripping from his body and his hair.

She could smell the stench of piss, of shit, of vomit, all around her as she felt that dampness under her feet and wondered whether it could be something to do with this guy.

And that wasn't even the most disturbing thing about this scene.

The man. His eyes. She could just about see the blood oozing from them as she stepped closer to him, cricket bat in hand.

But the closer she got to him, the more she realised that he wasn't just bleeding from his eyes.

There was something else about him.

Something different about him.

"Please," the man begged, whining like a baby, squealing like a pig. "Don't hurt me anymore. Please. Help me. Help me. Help..."

And maybe he carried on begging. He probably did.

But everything disappeared.

Everything faded all around Keira.

Because she saw the man's face flicker in the candlelight for just a second.

She saw his eyes.

Or rather...

The bloody spaces where his eyes once were.

Where his eyes were... there were two bloody holes.

Flesh trickled down his cheeks.

He gritted his teeth together in pain as he shook, as he quivered.

"Please," he gasped, snot oozing from his nostrils, drool from his lips. "Don't hurt me again. Please don't hurt me again."

And Keira wanted to care for this man. She wanted to put him at ease. She wanted to help him. Help him recover.

But...

What the hell could she do for a man in this state?

She reached a hand towards his shoulder. Placed her fingers against it. He was hot to the touch. And he jumped a bit, with pain or surprise, she wasn't sure.

"It's okay," she said.

"Please don't hurt me."

"I'm not here to hurt you. Ssh. It's okay. Everything... everything is going to be okay."

She kept her hand on his shoulder. She felt the sickness filling her body. Tasted the vomit lingering at the back of her throat.

She had to keep it together.

She had to be here for this man.

She had to look after him.

She had to keep him as comfortable as possible.

She kept on stroking his sweaty shoulder as the agonising tears of blood kept on pouring down his face. She kept on quietening him. Telling him it was going to be okay. Telling him everything was going to be okay.

She didn't know what else she could do for him. That rope around his neck. She could try cutting it. Yes. That's what she had to do. She had to cut him down. She couldn't let him suffer like this. She couldn't leave him sitting here like this. She needed to help him.

She swung the machete at the rope.

The rope cut away.

The man fell free, tumbled onto the floor, and landed with a thump and a cry.

She looked down at him, lying here in the foetal position, completely naked. She pitied him so much. This poor man. He'd been through so much. And how? What'd happened to him?

She reached down by his side. Sliced the ties around his wrists and his ankles.

And then she saw him roll up, curl even more into the foetal position, crying, sobbing, and yelping with every cry—every cry that must be agonising his empty eye sockets.

She crouched beside him. Stroked him some more. She realised her fingers were shaking. And she felt like she was on the brink of throwing up.

"It's okay," she said. "I'm here for you. I'm here."

"He took my family," he said.

Keira gulped. "Who took your family?"

"He took them. And then he... he told me he would come back for me. But he—he didn't want me to see what he was doing to my family. But I could hear it. I could hear it... arghhhh."

She heard his wail, and she felt empty. She felt cold. She felt dead. Completely dead.

"Please," he gasped. "Put me out of my misery. Please put me out of my misery."

Keira shook her head. "Who did this to you?"

"He did it. He took my family. He—"

"What was his name? Who did this to you?"

He looked up at her, then.

Stared in her direction with those empty, bloody eye sockets.

And then he said the words that sent a shiver right through her body.

"The man in the attic," he said.

She stood there.

Heart racing.

Shaking.

"What..." she started.

And that's when she heard it.

Right above her.

Banging.

Footsteps.

Someone was here.

SARAH

* * *

"You think we lost 'em?"

"I mean, we've lost them as much as we *can* lose them, I think."

"You could just say 'yes.' Just to lift spirits a bit."

"If I said 'yes,' I'd be lying."

"Sometimes a white lie isn't so bad."

"It is if it gets you killed."

Sarah stared back into the darkness of the woods. They were just outside those woods now. On a main road, in the middle of the darkness. Her leg hurt. She couldn't move without limping. That dog bite on her ankle. It was burning with agony, and it was getting even worse.

She couldn't hear any noises. Any groans. Anything like that. Just the hum of night. The call of animals, deep in the woods. Birds. Deer. That was a positive sign. If deer were around, then the chances of *infected* being around were slim, right?

But then again... she knew how the infected were changing.

She'd heard their calls. Their cries. She heard how they could imitate people.

Who was to say they couldn't imitate animals, too?

Who was to say they weren't just lulling her into a false sense of security?

She saw Carly standing next to her. Shaking her head. Kept on muttering under her breath. She looked really composed back at the caravan. Like she was in control. But now... now, she looked different. Very different.

She looked back into the woods with sadness.

She looked like she was lost.

She thought about that caravan. It was a real state. It stunk of sweat. And it was clammy as hell.

But to Carly... that place was home.

And she couldn't take that away from her.

"I'm sorry. About... what happened," Sarah said.

Carly looked around at her, then looked away quickly. Shook her head. Took a deep breath. "It's one of those things."

She didn't say it with any real conviction, though. She said it like she was trying to convince herself. Sarah didn't know whether to push her or whether to leave it at that.

But she found herself putting herself in this woman's shoes. She found herself imagining she was Carly. What would *she* want?

She gulped, tensed her fists, and sighed.

"It was your home."

"It was a stopgap," Carly snapped.

"It's okay to feel sad. About losing—"

"Why do you care so much all of a sudden?" Carly said.

She looked right at Sarah. And even though Sarah wasn't the best at deciphering emotions through facial expressions, she had to admit she looked pretty mad right now.

"I'm sorry," Carly said, looking away. She turned and started walking, Sarah right behind her.

"It's okay."

"It's just... the caravan. That was my first taste of freedom since..."

She stopped.

Stared, wide-eyed, off into the distance.

"Since when?" Sarah asked.

Carly gulped rather audibly. She cleared her throat. She sounded like she was going to say something. Like she was going to open up to Sarah. Let her in on her past. And then she sighed. "We need to find somewhere else to shelter."

A knot tightened in Sarah's stomach. Because she knew where she had to go. She had to go to that bridlepath again. And then, she had to try to trace Keira, Nisha, and Rufus' steps from there with that military group.

"Leonard," Sarah said.

Carly stopped. She looked down at the ground. Cleared her throat again.

"Where is he?"

"You don't want to know."

"If there's a chance he has my friends, then I—"

"Trust me," Carly snapped. "You're better off not knowing. If your friends were there, then—"

"One of my friends is a girl. And she can do what you can do."

Carly held her tongue, then. She didn't say another word. She just stared at Sarah. Wide-eyed.

"She can...?"

"She can hold back the infected. She was bitten, and she didn't turn. And... there's more to what she can do, too. The way she... collapses. The way the infected are when they're around her. It's almost as if she... as if she..."

"Can get inside their heads," Carly said.

Sarah nodded. Gulped. She wasn't sure how Carly knew what she was thinking. But she'd taken the words right out of her mouth.

Carly stood there. Picking at the bandage around her arm. She looked just past Sarah. Over her shoulder somewhere. Into the darkness. Like she was staring into a memory.

"It started on the first day," Carly said. "I... had a woman over."

"A woman?"

Carly narrowed her eyes. "Yes. A woman. Do I need to spell things out for you?"

"Sorry," Sarah said.

Carly shook her head. "I woke up. My bed was covered in blood. I got up. Searched for her. Found her crouched there on the landing. Spewing vomit and blood all over the place.

"And I remembered feeling so... guilty. Because the first thought in my head? The carpet was new. It'd cost loads. And she was messing it up."

Sarah couldn't help laughing a little, as inappropriate as she knew it might be. Mostly because it reminded her of a thought *she* might've had in such a situation. In such a context.

"I snapped out of it. I went over to try and help her. And... she bit me. Sunk her teeth into me. And... and I lashed out at her. I... I killed her. And I sat there. Holding my bitten arm. Trying to ease the blood flow. I sat there for so, so long. And even though I didn't understand what the bite meant right then... I still had this feeling deep inside me. This feeling that something was wrong. Very wrong."

Sarah thought back to her first days.

She thought back to Dean...

And to how much more recent that was than she cared to admit.

"It didn't take me long to realise what was happening outside. To hear the screams on the streets. To see the chaos. I saw people being bitten. I saw them turning. Some of them within seconds. And I still had this feeling within me. This sense within me. That I was going to turn. That I was going to change. But... I just didn't."

Sarah gulped. Everything Carly was saying. It matched up with what'd happened to Nisha. To the way Nisha had gone.

"And there was something else," Carly said.

Carly looked into her eyes. For just a second. Stared right into her eyes.

"What?" Sarah asked.

Carly opened her mouth. Took a deep breath. Closed her lips again.

"Carly," Sarah said. "What is it?"

She looked back at Sarah.

She swallowed a noisy lump in her throat once again.

And then she looked Sarah right in the eye and told her everything.

NISHA

* * *

Nisha watched the bad people getting closer to the window, and for some reason, for the first time since the first day, something felt... different.

They were all running towards her. These figures. Three that she could see. Running fast through the darkness.

And she could feel her heart pumping faster in her chest. And it was pumping so fast that she was finding it hard to breathe, and her legs were getting all shaky and wobbly like jelly.

She stood there and looked out the window, knowing she needed to find Keira and Rufus. She needed to tell them about the bad people. She needed to warn them about the bad people.

And then they needed to hide somewhere.

Anywhere.

Because these bad people.

They were running towards the house.

They were getting closer and closer.

She turned around, and she started to walk across the room

towards the door Keira had gone through when she felt a pain in her belly.

And then she saw a flash in her eyes.

Someone there.

Someone standing right there. Right in front of her.

The Girl.

No.

No, a *snake*.

A thick, dark snake, staring right at her, its breath so warm and smelly, and bats all flying around it, and—

We're close we're close we're close—

Why was she thinking those words?

What was happening?

She held her chest, and she stood up again, as tall as she could. But her tummy was aching so bad. And her knees were so weak. And her chest was so tight.

And those words in her head.

They weren't like the woman's voice.

They were...

Something different.

Some*one* different.

Just stay there stay there it'll all be over everything will be over she won't hurt anyone again Mother won't hurt anyone again Mother won't...

And Nisha couldn't understand it, but she felt this urge.

She felt this certainty. Deep inside her.

This absolute certainty.

Certainty that she needed to get away from here fast.

And that she had to find that girl, wherever she was, fast.

They couldn't wait here and rest anymore.

They needed to get away from here.

Because something about these bad people felt different from the normal bad people.

Something about these bad people seemed *scarier* than the normal bad people.

And there was something about these bad people that made her think she couldn't escape them like she could the other bad people.

She turned around and ran to the door. She grabbed it. Turned the handle.

But she could feel scratching in her ears and filling her head.

And she could taste...

Blood.

Blood, and sick, and—

Almost there almost got you almost over almost all over almost—

She gritted her teeth.

She felt like she couldn't move properly. Like she was wearing a really heavy backpack, and it was weighing down heavy on her shoulders, and she could barely move, she could barely breathe, she could barely think.

She just had to get out of here.

She just had to get to Keira.

She just had to—

Splitting pain.

An explosion. Right through her chest.

She fell to the floor. Held her chest. Her heart was beating so fast. Racing. Thumping, harder and harder and harder.

She crouched there. On her knees. She could feel her head getting heavier. She could taste the blood getting stronger. No. No, this was bad. It was bad because it reminded her of the times she'd passed out, and she couldn't wake up again, and she'd had the dreams. She'd had all the dreams.

She felt like if she passed out again, if she had those dreams again, this time, she wouldn't be able to wake up from them.

She sat there on her knees, staring down at the floor, and as weak as she felt, as hard as the thought of standing up felt... she pushed herself up to her feet.

She looked around even though she didn't want to look around because looking around scared her.

And then she saw them.

They were right at the window.

And then were banging at the window.

Smashing the window open.

Climbing in.

And the taste in her mouth and the heaviness in her head was getting stronger and—

She turned around, lowered the handle, ran out into the hall, opened her mouth, and let out a noise.

A noise that felt like a scream.

She felt a tight grip around her throat.

She felt herself try to breathe, but she couldn't breathe; she couldn't let any breath in.

She saw the snake.

She saw...

No.

No, that couldn't be...

The snake.

The bats.

The person.

Right in the middle of them all.

Looking right at her.

Standing in the middle of the darkest darkness she'd ever seen.

Blood oozing down her face.

From her rolled-back eyes.

Blubbering blood.

Smiling.

No...

She looked at her as she stood there, frozen in the dark.

And then she felt the real hands—the hands of the bad people—grabbing her, pushing her down to the floor, and pinning her down and...

KEIRA

* * *

Keira heard the banging up the stairs, and her whole body went numb.

She stood in the candlelit darkness of the cellar. Opposite her, she saw this naked man.

Lying on the dusty concrete floor.

Eyes gouged out.

Crying.

Whimpering.

"Don't let him come back," he gasped. "Don't let the man from the attic come back."

And hearing those words. Then hearing that banging upstairs. Nisha? It was impossible to tell.

But hearing Rufus growling and whining.

And standing there in the darkness...

Keira knew she needed to get upstairs. She needed to get to Nisha. She needed to make sure she was okay.

She looked back at the man as a shiver crept down her spine.

She would help him. She would come back for him. She wasn't going to leave him like this.

"I'll be back for you," Keira said.

The man looked up, crying, shaking. Snot oozing down his lips. "Please don't leave me."

"I'm not leaving you," Keira said. The weight of the guilt growing stronger in her stomach. "I'll... I'll be right back for you—"

She heard a bang.

A shriek.

Upstairs.

She turned around.

Her body turned cold.

Something was happening up there.

She ran up the stairs as fast as she could. Rufus ran beside her, barking as they ascended. She gripped her cricket bat tight. Nisha. She shouldn't have left Nisha in the lounge. She shouldn't have let her slip from her sight.

She ran towards the door to the cupboard under the stairs. The man screamed behind her, cried out in fear, in pain, or a mixture of both.

She heard glass smashing.

She heard gasping.

She heard footsteps racing through the house.

Someone was here.

The infected?

Fuck.

She was about to find out.

She clenched the cricket bat.

Then she grabbed the handle.

She'll be okay.

Everything will be okay.

She had to believe that.

She turned the handle.

Yanked the door open.

She saw Nisha standing right in front of her.

Her eyes were wide.

She looked like she was crying.

She looked...

Scared.

She glanced up at Keira.

And before Keira could even register a thing—before even Nisha could apparently register a thing—she tumbled to the floor.

An infected man.

Pinning her down.

Screaming at her.

Blood spouting from his lips.

A nasty bite wound right across his bald skull.

Keira couldn't even think.

She could only react in one way, as that man pinned Nisha down, as he held her to the floor, pressing his knee right down on her skinny body so hard that Keira worried it might just split to pieces.

Her instincts to protect overwhelmed her.

She lunged forward.

She swung the cricket bat right across the infected man's head.

It hit his head with a thump and a crack. Blood splattered up all over her hands. She could taste it, metallic against her lips.

She yanked the bat away.

And then, as the man rolled off Nisha, yelping with pitiful agony, Keira went to swing it at his head again.

She slammed it against the side of his head.

Cracked it against his temple.

Dug it in so hard that the man couldn't shake himself free of it no matter how hard he tried.

She pushed it in deep.

Then she tried to pull it away.

But it was stuck.

It was stuck, and another infected was racing around the corner of the lounge.

She tried to yank it free.

Tried to pull it away.

But it was stuck.

Completely fucking stuck.

She let go of the bat before the infected woman could reach her.

She grabbed Nisha's hand.

Dragged her to her feet.

Stumbled back towards the door to the cupboard under the stairs as this infected woman raced towards her.

They had to get away.

They had to get back down into the cellar.

That was the only place they could go.

They had to hide.

She dragged Nisha back.

Pulled open the door.

Went to slam it shut—

The infected woman barged it open immediately.

Keira stood there in the opening to these stairs.

She heard the man screaming downstairs.

"Please! No! Don't hurt me! No!"

She squeezed Nisha's hand, and she felt gratitude—immense gratitude—that Nisha couldn't hear a thing right now.

"It's okay," she muttered as the infected woman launched towards them. "Everything's going to be..."

It all happened so fast.

The bat in the infected man's skull, right by the door.

Someone appearing.

Right there.

Yanking it away.

Then swinging it across this woman's skull.

Right down the middle.

Shattering it immediately with a heavy thunk.

Keira stood there. Holding Nisha's hand. Rufus barking beside her.

Blood splattering from the infected woman's head.

The bat rising.

The infected woman falling to her feet.

And then she saw him.

A man.

Standing there in the darkness.

He looked soaking wet. Like he'd been out in the rain for a long time.

"Come on," he said. Hard to make him out in this darkness. Hard to see his face properly. "We need to get out of here. We need to go. Now. Right now!"

Keira looked down the stairs. Down towards the screaming man in the cellar.

"Did you hear me?" the man who'd saved her shouted. "No time to stick around right now. There's more of them."

"I can't leave him..."

She heard a window smashing somewhere.

Heard the screaming growing louder.

Saw the man in front of her turning around, looking over his shoulder, then back at her.

"Fuck," he said. "It's now or never. I'm... I'm sorry, but it's now or never."

Keira looked down the stairs.

She pictured that man. Lying there naked. Alone. With his bloodied, gouged eyes.

She remembered the fear in his voice.

The desperation, after all he'd suffered.

"Please don't hurt me. Please don't leave me."

She heard those words, and then she looked around at this man.

And at Rufus.

And then at Nisha, right beside her.

You can't save everybody.

She heard the infected racing through the living room.

Smelled the earthiness growing stronger, stronger.

Rufus's barking getting louder.

"I'm sorry," Keira said. "I'm so sorry."

And then she stepped out of the cupboard under the stairs, yanked the door shut, and ran through the house with this mystery stranger, Nisha by her side, Rufus by her side, and the infected close behind.

Deep in the bowels of the house, she heard the poor man's screams.

SARAH

* * *

Sarah stared at Carly and tried to process everything she'd just told her.

It was late. Dark. The pair had just spent the last forever running through the woods. Trying to get away from the mass of infected that broke into Carly's caravan. Which, with a leg that a monster dog hadn't long ago savaged, wasn't exactly a piece of cake.

They'd made it out of there. Found themselves in the middle of nowhere. Which bothered Sarah deeply. She really rather desperately wanted to locate Keira, Nisha, and Rufus. It'd been a long time since she'd seen them. And somehow, retracing her steps back to the bridleway on which she'd lost them didn't sound like the easiest of tasks.

But after what Carly just told her... it felt like the most urgent of tasks.

The implications of what Carly just told her.

About what happened to her.

About what she could do.

And about...

Leonard.

Leonard and the military group.

She ran through everything. Saw the thoughts flickering through her head. Their implications. What they meant.

"Are you okay?" Carly said. "You look like you've just been hit by a bus."

Sarah cleared her throat. Shook her head. "In a way, I kind of have."

Carly nodded. "Yeah. I can imagine."

What Carly told her.

What it all meant.

The secrets.

The secrets she had kept for so long.

And what those same secrets might mean for Nisha...

"We can't just stay here," Sarah said.

"No. You're right about that. But your leg's fucked."

A twinge shot up Sarah's leg the second Carly brought her attention to it. The dog bite. Getting even worse. Probably hadn't helped that she'd spent ages limping through the woods, fleeing the infected.

But when Sarah said those words... she had something very specific in mind.

Because if what Carly just told her was true... there was only one place she could go.

She started walking. It hurt. But she knew she had to walk. She had to find out where they were. And then she had to find her way to Nisha. To Keira. To Rufus.

Because if they were at Leonard's place...

"What are you doing?" Carly asked.

"I need to find them."

"After everything I just told you?"

"*Especially* after everything you just told me," Sarah said.

Carly shook her head. "Are you insane?"

She gulped. Wiped her damp fringe from her forehead. "I'm sorry. What you went through. I'm sorry for everything you've been through. For everything you've just told me."

"I don't want your fucking sympathy," Carly said. "I want you to listen to what I'm telling you. You go after them... you're going to die. They're already dead, Sarah—"

"I can't believe that. Not until I know for sure."

Carly sighed. "I've tried to help you. I've tried to warn you. For some reason, I've told you more than I've told anyone."

"And I appreciate that. I respect that."

"I sense a 'but' coming..."

Sarah tried her best to form a sentence that sounded as coherent but also as empathetic as possible. "These people. They are my friends."

"I've told you—"

"And despite what you've told me. Despite what you claim you've *seen*... I can't just give up on them."

She looked at Carly.

Then she walked right past her.

She didn't have time to think.

She didn't have time to speculate.

She had to find them.

And she had to find them fast.

"Even after what I told you about The Girl?"

Sarah stopped.

The words spun around her head.

The Girl.

The Girl Carly told her about.

The things she'd told her.

The things she could do.

The things she'd *seen*...

"You go there," Carly said. "You go to the North Lancs Barracks. You go after her. And you go after... after Leonard. And it doesn't end well for you. It doesn't end well for anyone."

Sarah shook her head. "I want to believe what you're saying."

"But you can't. Because it sounds too far-fetched. Because it sounds batshit crazy."

"The world we live in is far-fetched. The world we live in is batshit crazy. But... it's not a foregone conclusion that they've made it to Leonard's. There are other military types on the road. You've seen them. I've seen them. I have to go back to where I lost them. I have to try my best to find them. They... they are the best friends I have ever had. And they don't even know it. And I will never give up on them. But I understand if you can't make this journey with me."

Carly stared at her. Her eyes glowing in the moonlight. A deer calling somewhere in the distance. Up the street, something shuffling in the breeze.

"I understand," Sarah said. "After... what you went through. And after what you've seen. But I can't give up on them. And even less than ever, after what you told me. I have to find them. I have to stop them. That's... that's on me."

Carly opened her mouth. She looked like she was going to say something else to Sarah. Something to slap her to her senses. And in all honesty, Sarah had to admit she rather *wanted* her to. Because the Sarah of weeks ago would not have gone running after some people she, in the grand scheme of things, barely even knew.

But...

No.

The Sarah of a few weeks ago wasn't the Sarah of today.

And when Carly spoke, she said something Sarah didn't expect.

"How can you be so... selfless?"

Sarah blushed at those words. Selflessness was something she'd never been accused of in her life.

But the more she thought about it... the more she thought

about Carly's words... the more she realised that, logically, she was acting rather selflessly indeed.

She just wasn't sure how to feel about it.

She gulped and took a deep breath of the cool night air as rain pummelled down from above.

"I have to do whatever I can," she said. "For my friends."

Carly nodded. She stood there. Staring at Sarah. It looked like she still wanted to say something. Like she had unspoken words on her mind.

"And what about the truth?" Carly asked her.

She thought about the truth.

She thought about what Carly had told her.

Everything she had told her.

She thought about the implications of what she'd told her.

She thought about how much danger Nisha was in if she made it to this Leonard's place.

And then she thought about the next thing she'd told her.

The thing that... didn't make sense.

The thing that filled her with fear.

The thing that she just couldn't wrap her head around.

That she just couldn't believe.

Nisha is already dead.

If she makes it to Leonard's place, we're all as good as dead.

And if you find her before she does... she's better off dead.

KEIRA

* * *

Keira looked back towards the house, and even though they were a long way away, she was sure she could still hear that poor eyeless man trapped in the cellar screaming.

But she had another problem to contend with.

And that was that her, Nisha, and Rufus weren't alone.

The man was called Theo. He had short, dark hair. Pale skin. Quite muscular. He wasn't unattractive. Which seemed like an entirely inappropriate thought to have, given the circumstances, but human nature was human nature, right?

He'd saved them all from that godforsaken house. The place where it all went to hell. He'd bailed them out when it looked like all hope was lost. And that deserved some gratitude.

But Keira knew better than to blindly trust any stranger. Even if he *had* just saved their lives.

She stood in the middle of the country lane that it felt like she'd been walking on forever. Theo stood in front of her. She held on to Nisha's hand tightly. She'd had a close run-in with the infected. For whatever reason, she hadn't been able to stop that group from attacking her.

Maybe her abilities, for want of a better word, were waning.

Or maybe the infected were changing.

Getting stronger...

She held her hand. Rufus stood at her side. Panting. Even he seemed shaken up by what just happened at the house. And it took a lot to unsettle him.

But he didn't seem to mind their new companion. Which, if the good-nature-detecting instincts of dogs weren't overblown, had to be a good thing.

Right?

"How did you find us?" Keira asked.

Theo took a deep breath. Rain fell from above. A cool breeze made the hairs on Keira's arms stand on end.

"I was just passing," Theo said.

"Just passing? In the middle of the night?"

"Yes."

"And, what, you hear shit going down, so you just throw yourself in there? Risk your life for a bunch of people you don't know?"

Theo shrugged. "It looks that way, doesn't it?"

Keira shook her head. It didn't add up in any way. But at the same time... he kind of had a point.

He'd appeared. Out of nowhere.

He'd saved her. Saved Nisha. Saved Rufus.

They owed their lives to him.

Why did she still feel so sceptical?

And why did she get the feeling she'd seen him somewhere before? Like there was something oddly familiar about him?

She thought back to the man in the cellar.

Those bloody, gouged eye sockets.

The snot oozing down his chin as he lay there, naked, in the foetal position.

"Don't let him hurt me... the man from the attic..."

"The man we left back there," Keira said. "He—"

"We couldn't have saved him."

"What makes you say that?"

"If we'd tried to save him, we would've got trapped there. We didn't have a choice."

Keira shook her head. Again, she didn't *want* it to make sense. But it did.

"It's just..." she started.

Theo looked right at her. His face silhouetted in the darkness. "What?"

She took a deep breath. Sighed. "The man. In the cellar. The state he was in. Someone... did that to him. And he said something, too. Something about a man. In the attic."

Theo didn't speak for a moment. They all just stood there. Together. Silent.

"Oh," he said. "You think *I'm* the man in the attic?"

The way he said it sent a shiver down Keira's spine.

"Well. You did appear out of nowhere—"

"Soaked to the skin."

"What?"

"When I found you. I was soaked to the skin. Clearly wasn't a very good attic to hide away in if I was so drenched, hmm?"

Keira shook her head. She didn't like this guy's confidence. It bordered on cocky.

But at the same time... she had to admit she remembered him dripping wet when he found them.

He rubbed the back of his head. "Look. I don't have anything to prove to you. I helped you out of there. As far as I'm concerned, that's my good deed for the week. But if you lot want to take your chances on the road now, well, good luck. Knock yourself out."

He turned around. Started walking back in the direction Keira had originally come from.

And then he stopped.

Just like that, he stopped in the darkness and in the rain.

"But just one thing," he said.

He turned around. Slowly.

Looked right at Keira.

"You're going to want to avoid wandering up this road," he said. "If those mad fuckers don't get you first, the looters will. Real bad group stationed right in the middle of the way. Absolutely no way two women pass through there untouched." He looked down at Rufus, then. "I hear they like dogs, though. In their stew."

Rufus whined.

Theo nodded at her again. Then turned away. Kept on walking away down that road. Shit. That'd put a real spanner in the works. What the hell was she supposed to do now?

"What do you suggest?" Keira asked.

The man stopped again. Laughed a little. "You want my suggestion?"

"That's what it sounds like, doesn't it?"

He shrugged. "If I were you, I wouldn't head north. End of story."

"But if... if we *have* to head north."

Theo didn't speak for quite a few seconds. As time stretched on, Keira wondered whether he'd forgotten her question altogether.

And then, finally, he answered.

"I know a way," he said.

"You do?"

"It's not guaranteed," he said. "It's not perfect. But... it's something."

Keira stood there, holding Nisha's hand.

She stood there. Rufus right beside her.

She stood there.

Staring at this mysterious man, shrouded by darkness.

"I guess the question is, do you trust me?" he asked.

She looked around into the darkness of the road stretching behind them.

Then she looked back at Theo.

Right at this man drenched in such mystery.

This man who seemed to revel in this mystery.

A man who had saved her life.

"I'd be an idiot to trust you," Keira said. "And you'd be an idiot to trust me."

Theo smiled. "Good answer."

"But if you know a way... then I think you should tell us."

Theo was silent for a few seconds again. He stood there, smiling, as the moon lit his scarred face just a little brighter.

Then, after what felt like another eternity...

"Have you ever been in a sewer, Keira?"

"I can't say I have."

A smile crept across his face. "Then prepare to check that one off your bucket list."

SETH

* * *

Seth watched the pretty people up the road standing there in the moonlight, and he wanted to be friends with them so, so much.

He could see them. The little girl so cute, so precious. The dog looked like he enjoyed strokes, playing, long walks, and having his ball thrown for him.

And he saw the lady, too.

The lady.

The lady who made him feel happy.

The lady who made him feel special.

The lady, who he wanted to be friends with more than anyone he'd ever met.

The lady who made him warm inside.

The lady he'd waited so long for.

So many years for.

The lady who made him warm in his trousers...

He remembered what Mum said to him when she found him rubbing his Bad Part to a black and white photograph of Aunt

Nora when he was younger. She'd bent him over, and she'd spanked him hard.

But the bad thing?

It didn't matter how hard she spanked him.

His Bad Part wouldn't go down.

It wouldn't go soft.

And then the fireworks went off inside him, and...

He remembered the way she'd taken him into the bathroom. The water steaming hot.

The way she'd held him tight and dangled him over it, dangled his Bad Part over it.

You can't spread your evil; I won't let you spread your evil...

And then he remembered the burning pain.

He was reminded of that burning pain right now.

Because looking at the lady, at the beautiful lady, it made his Bad Part hard.

And when his Bad Part got hard... the most intense, crippling pain filled his body.

But it was going to be okay with the Lady.

Everything was going to be okay with the Lady.

He watched her climb down the ladder, and then he saw...

Him.

A cold feeling crept up the back of his neck. He felt his jaw tighten. Heard voices circling around his spinning head.

He was always there.

When he wanted to make friends, when he wanted to ask a lady out for a drink and to a restaurant and then just back to his place to cuddle and be happy, *he* was always there.

He watched him hold her hand.

He watched him help her down the ladders into that tunnel in the ground.

He watched them all disappear down there into the darkness, and he felt rage.

Because they were his people.

They were his friends.

And that Lady was his.

He thought back to the man in the house. The one in the cellar. He hadn't been trying to hurt him. He'd just been trying to help him. He'd waited in the attic. Hid in there. He'd watched him looking after his wife. His children. Protecting them.

And that's what he wanted. More than anything, he just wanted to feel like he could look after other people, too.

It took Seth a long time before he mustered up the courage to climb the stairs. To introduce himself to them. Because they seemed so warm. They seemed so kind.

But... the kids.

And the lady.

They screamed when they saw him.

And then the man started hitting him, and it all got out of hand, and he wanted to make them quiet, he wanted to...

He hit them. He tied them up.

And then...

The man didn't want him to watch what Seth was doing to his family. To his wife. To his children.

Not like Seth had been made to watch Mum do all those things, all those years ago.

Things with other men.

Things by herself.

Things with knives.

Things with scissors.

Things with—

The Bad Part.

He closed his eyes as tears flowed down his cheeks. And for a moment, for just a moment, he wished he could be like *him*.

He wished he could have real friends.

He wished people didn't tease him, mock him, and look at him like he was weird.

He wished they didn't run away from him.

Because when they ran away from him, it made him sad. So sad.

When they ran away from him, it made him angry.

When they ran away from him... it made him want to make them quiet.

So he could spend time with them.

Time they couldn't run away from.

He watched them walk down the ladders, and he heard a voice in his head.

Don't do this, Seth. I've got this. They trust me, see? They trust me. We can both be friends with them. It doesn't have to be this way...

And then Seth felt the burning jealousy, the intense rage, as *he* climbed down the ladder last and descended into the darkness.

He waited.

Waited in the shadows.

Waited for his moment.

His moment to try and be friends with them.

To try and be *more* than friends with the lady.

Because she was so beautiful. And he loved her. And he wanted a family with her. And to have lots and lots of kids with her.

Don't do this.

Don't do this.

Don't...

And then he took a deep breath, and when he was sure he was in the clear, he let himself down that ladder.

Into the darkness.

Right behind them.

SARAH

* * *

"And what about the truth?" Carly asked.

Sarah stood in the middle of the road, in the depths of darkness, and she thought about what Carly had told her.

Nisha is already dead.

If she makes it to Leonard's place, we're all as good as dead.

And if you find her before she does... she's better off dead.

Her head spun. She still couldn't wrap her head around those words. She still couldn't accept what Carly had told her.

Because it sounded like madness. Craziness.

How could Carly understand a thing about Nisha when she hadn't even met her?

But then she remembered the other things Carly had told her.

The other things she'd said to her.

And the more she thought about those revelations, those claims, the more her sense of uneasiness grew.

"I appreciate what you told me," Sarah said. Trying to remain as diplomatic as possible.

"I don't much care whether you appreciate it or not," Carly said. "What I care about is what that lunatic is going to do if he gets his hands on another person like me. On another person like The Girl. And on another person like... like this Nisha."

"So your suggestion is to *destroy* her?" Sarah asked.

Carly rolled her eyes. Turned around. "Don't say it like that."

But that was exactly what Carly was suggesting.

She'd told her that in the early days, she'd found herself in this Leonard's camp. That things were different there. They were paranoid. Deeply paranoid about stepping outside. About breathing the air. Because the infection, it spread through the air.

And Carly told her how she trusted this Leonard.

She told her how she looked up to him in those early days.

How *everyone* looked up to him.

And then she told her about the dreams.

The dreams that she was... separate from herself somehow. Only over time, she realised those dreams were getting stronger. They were getting clearer.

And then she realised she was seeing through the eyes of the infected.

As nonsensical as it sounded, as baffling as it was for Sarah to believe... Carly claimed she could disappear inside the heads of the infected.

That she could see the world through their eyes.

But there was something else.

Something even greater than that.

"If Nisha is like me, if she's like... if she's like the other girl. Then they cannot be together."

"So you keep saying," Sarah said.

"Leonard wants to use them," Carly said. "Don't you understand? He's like a fucking tinpot dictator with a nuclear arsenal. And if he has another one with him... he can train them to make the infected do what he wants. Exactly what he wants."

Sarah shook her head as she stared at Carly, standing there in the darkness.

"I appreciate it's a lot," Carly said. "I really fucking respect that. But you need to believe me when I say she can't make it there."

"But that doesn't explain why she has to die," Sarah said.

Carly opened her mouth. She paused, just for a second. Looked like she was going to say something, but was torn over whether to elaborate or not.

Then she just shook her head. Turned around.

"You can't just leave me hanging like that," Sarah said.

"There's things you can't possibly begin to understand."

"You know, for someone who prides herself on her incredibly straight-talking approach to life, you aren't half cryptic."

Carly shook her head. Raised a hand. "If you'd seen the things I'd seen—"

"I'd be calling for the death of an innocent child, too. I get it."

Carly stopped, then, which was just as well. Sarah's ankle might be causing her a lot of grief right now, and her entire body might be causing her the same amount of grief as it always did. But she felt close to snapping at Carly for her suggestions about Nisha.

"I know it seems insensitive."

"'Seems insensitive?' The murder of a child?"

"The power she has. The power both of them have..."

"And what about you?"

"What about me?"

"You said it yourself. You're just like them. You managed to get away from Leonard. By your own logic, should you need to die, too?"

Carly shook her head. She tutted under her breath like she was disappointed at Sarah's suggestion. "You still don't get it, do you?"

"Then tell me what I don't get. Tell me what I don't understand. Because right now, respectfully, you sound crazy. Respectfully."

She took a deep breath. Sighed.

She walked right up to Sarah.

Looked right into her eyes.

"I'm different. You're right. I'm powerful. I can do things. Correct."

A pause. The tension of the moment hanging in the air.

"But The Girl... and this... Nisha, as you call her..."

A knot tightened in Sarah's stomach.

"You're not understanding, are you?" Carly said.

"I'm not understanding because you aren't fucking telling me—"

"You're not understanding because you don't *want* to see."

"See *what?*"

Carly looked deep into Sarah's eyes.

Half-smiled as the night illuminated her face.

"What 'Mother' really is. How it spreads. And who it lives inside. Because you don't *want* to see it. And you don't *want* to accept it yourself. Do you, Sarah?"

Sarah's skin turned cold.

She didn't get it.

She didn't understand it.

It didn't make any sense.

But it scared her.

It scared her because a part of her wondered if she *did* understand, and she *was* just resisting the truth.

The inevitable truth.

"What..." she started.

And right on cue, she heard something.

Not the shriek of the infected.

Not the ravenous snarls of the less fortunate.

Not the footsteps of the frenzied slamming against the concrete, splashing through the puddles.

No, she heard something different entirely.
From over her shoulder, Sarah heard an engine.
She turned around.
Saw car headlights beaming towards her.
She didn't know who it was.
She didn't know what they wanted.
But one thing was for sure.
They weren't alone.

NISHA

***

Nisha climbed down the ladder into the dark and smelly place called the "sewer", and she kept her eyes on the weird man at all times.

She didn't like him. She wasn't trying to be mean or anything. She knew it was bad to make your mind up about people based on their appearance or what you first thought of them. And this man *had* been quite nice. He'd helped her. Saved her from the bad people. The ones she didn't feel strong enough to hold back.

And he'd helped Keira and Rufus, too. He'd helped them get away from that house. And now he was leading them somewhere so they could get to the North Lancs Barracks place, as Keira wrote it.

So, how bad could he be?

But there was something strange about him. There was something about him that made her feel weird inside. Like how Uncle Sammy used to make her feel before he got arrested for things that Dad said she was too young to understand.

He might've helped her.

But there was nothing about this man that made her feel comfortable. That made her feel safe.

Everything about him made her feel just like Uncle Sammy used to make her feel.

She held Keira's hand. It was so dark down here. It made her feel scared and sick. It was so cold, too, so deep down. And it smelled so bad. Like the worst toilets in the world.

But as she walked along the slippery ground, further into the dark, right next to the even darker river of smelly water at their side, even though she was cold and even though she was scared, she had this feeling deep inside her chest and her tummy where she usually felt the butterflies that she was going exactly where she needed to go.

The voice was gone. The voice of the lady in her head. And weirdly... she felt down here like she couldn't do the weird thing with the bad people anymore. Like she couldn't... *connect* with them.

Because that's what it'd felt like before. Like she could connect with them.

And even though she hadn't really noticed it at the time... now that feeling was *gone*, she noticed it more than ever.

It was like she was carrying something really heavy. Like when David Cooper jumped on her shoulders at school, and she tried to walk around with him there.

Only she couldn't walk.

She fell.

And he landed on her and knocked the wind out of her, and she couldn't breathe, and it made the butterflies in her tummy and her chest fly so fast, and so hard, and...

It was gone now. All of it was gone.

She thought back to the house. The bad people in there. The ones who pinned her down. The ones who tried to bite her. Was she different now? And by that, she meant... was she the same as everyone else now?

And in a way, even though that was scarier, that's kind of what she wanted all along, wasn't it?

She wanted to be the same as everyone else.

She was tired of being different.

She just wanted to be...

Normal.

She felt a squeeze against her hand. Looked up. Saw Keira looking down at her. It was hard to see her face in the dark. But she wanted to think that she was smiling. The way she'd squeezed her hand. It *felt* like she was smiling, anyway.

She looked down and saw Rufus. And... again, it was hard to see, 'cause it was pitch black down here, but she swore she could see him wagging his tail.

And that made her happy, too. It made her so happy. 'Cause for so long, Rufus had been scared of her. He'd looked at her like he was afraid of her.

And now he looked happy to see her again.

She looked around at the man walking ahead.

Even though it was dark and smelly, Nisha wondered why people couldn't stay down here. Maybe there were bad germs down here. But it would be one good way to stay away from the bad people, wouldn't it?

She watched the man walking along, holding this little flame thing in his hands that people used to light their cigarettes, barely lighting the darkness around him.

She looked at him, and she felt like Rufus must've felt when he looked at her and knew something was wrong with her.

But they were still following him.

Because it felt like the right thing to do.

They walked further through this tunnel. Into the darkness. And when they'd been walking for a while, the man stopped. He was trying to get through a door. But he couldn't get through it. It was stuck. And he was saying things to Keira. Things she couldn't hear. And it looked like they were arguing about something, and—

A flicker.

A flicker in her tummy.

A whisper in her chest.

Like words in her head.

Bouncing along in the wind like autumn leaves.

Close close close...

She turned around.

Turned around while Keira and the man were shouting at each other, arguing with each other.

Looked back down the tunnel.

Into the dark.

Close close close close close...

She looked down there into the dark.

She felt the darkness all around her.

She felt the silence all around her.

And then—

A blast.

A blast of something in her ears, so loud, like she was being punched and hit and—

White.

White and black light flashed across her eyes.

Her body tightened up.

She tasted sick.

She tasted blood.

She tasted—

Nothing.

She was back. Back in the darkness. Back in the tunnel. But the butterflies. They were fluttering around her tummy now.

Unless they weren't butterflies.

Unless they were...

Bats.

She looked down the tunnel into the dark when suddenly she noticed something.

Keira's grip on her hand.

Loosening.

She looked around.

Saw Rufus.

Standing there.

Staring down the tunnel.

Barking.

Kicking back against the sewer floor.

She saw the man looking down the tunnel.

She saw Keira looking down the tunnel.

And then she turned around and in the darkness, and through all the horrible smells... she smelled the worst smell of all.

Earthiness.

SARAH

* * *

Sarah saw the headlights glowing in the distance.

It was a car. Driving down the road, hurtling towards them. She felt like the proverbial rabbit right now, staring wide-eyed at those headlights as they hurried towards her, towards Carly. She'd seen plenty of cars abandoned on the side of the road over the last few weeks. And she'd seen a few people attempting to drive, trying to navigate their way through the sea of debris.

But this car. In the middle of the night. Hurtling down the road towards them.

It scared her.

In some ways, the unpredictability of other people was even scarier than the relative predictability of the infected.

And it wasn't like they weren't very bloody scary.

She stood there in the road. Totally still. Frozen. Watching those lights race towards her.

"We need to get off the road," Carly said.

No shit, Sherlock.

She ran across the road towards the trees. She couldn't run for long. Her run soon turned to a walk, which progressed to a limp. She looked down at her leg. Blood seeping through Carly's bandages. The dog bite. Getting even worse. Felt like it was itching and like it was burning now, too. Damn it. Infection was the last thing she wanted right now. Not even the dramatic kind of infection, either. Just bog-standard old-world shit.

She stumbled into the trees, by the side of the road, as the car raced closer towards them, when suddenly she heard a cry.

She turned around.

Saw Carly lying there on the road. On her knees. Hands on the ground. She'd fallen. She'd fallen, and the car was getting closer and...

Sarah limped back towards her. She knew it was crazy. If Carly didn't get to her feet fast, if she didn't get out of the way... they were going to be hit. They were both going to be hit by this car.

And Sarah could think of few worse things than being hit by a car and left broken on the side of the road while the infected circled, closer and closer.

She grabbed Carly by her arms. "Come on. Get to your feet."

Carly shook her head. Winced. "My ankle."

"Your ankle can wait," Sarah said. "You'll have far worse issues if you don't get to your feet right now."

She held her tight.

Looked around.

The car.

The headlights.

Racing faster and faster towards them both.

She gritted her teeth.

She turned around to Carly.

She saw her lying there on her knees, wincing in agony.

"I'm sorry," Sarah said.

And then she yanked her to her feet.

Carly let out a cry as the pressure shifted onto her feet.

Sarah dragged her from the road.

And as the car hurtled closer, her drag turned into a stumble, and a fall, and...

She fell to the road.

Slammed her head against the hard concrete.

Tasted blood.

But Carly landed beside her.

The car...

Whizzed past.

She felt the air blast against it as it flew by. So fast it actually felt like it'd hit her.

But it hadn't hit her.

It hadn't hit Carly.

They were both lying on the road.

They were both safe.

They were both... okay.

Or at least as okay as they could be.

Sarah looked around at the car as it flew past. And as she squinted at it, she realised it wasn't a normal car at all. It was a military vehicle. Some kind of military vehicle. She wasn't sure how to feel about that. Only that it made her feel uneasy. That was her gut instinct. The military made her feel uneasy.

She looked around at Carly. Saw her lying beside her. Puffing her lips. "Shit," she said.

Sarah took a deep breath. Nodded. "Yeah." It was about all she could say. All she could manage.

She stood up. Brushed herself down. Helped Carly to her feet gently.

"My ankle," Carly winced. "I must've... rolled it. Fuck, it's sore."

"Being mowed down by a car would've been a whole lot more sore. Come on. Let's... let's get to the..."

She heard it suddenly.

Right ahead of her.

Deep in the woods.

A scream.

She stood there. Shaking. Heart racing.

That scream.

It could belong to someone.

Or it could belong to...

Another scream.

To the right.

And then another somewhere further to the right.

Then another to the left.

And then another.

And the longer these cries went on, the more the confirmation dawned in Sarah's mind.

"Infected," Carly said, speaking Sarah's thoughts aloud.

Sarah turned around. But her own leg was hurting now. Throbbing. And the pain was radiating even further and further up her lower leg and into her upper thigh. Fuck. This wasn't good. This wasn't at all what she needed right now.

And Carly. She wasn't moving well, either.

Neither of them was moving well at all.

But they had to.

They had to get away.

They had to *try*.

She limped across the road as the screams grew louder, as the shrieks intensified, and as behind her, the sound of footsteps hammered through the woods, closer and closer towards them both.

"We can do this," she muttered. As painful as she found those empty, self-reassuring promises. "We can make it."

She staggered further across the road, clinging to Carly, when suddenly she heard something else.

And saw something, too.

The headlights.

The headlights of the military vehicle.

They were driving towards them both again.

Hurtling towards them both.

They were coming back for them.

Whoever the hell they were... they were coming back for them.

KEIRA

* * *

Keira heard the shrieks echoing through the sewer, and her stomach sank.

It was pitch black. It smelled like shit. And she was stuck at this doorway, deep in the pit of the sewer. The bloke she was with, Theo, he was trying to lower the handle, trying to break through.

But the door wasn't budging at all.

They were trapped down here.

She held Nisha's hand tight. She looked down beside her. Saw Rufus growling. Then heard him barking. And his barks were so loud down here in these confines. Echoing their way through this tunnel.

Drawing the infected closer and closer towards them.

"I thought you said it was safe down here," Keira shouted.

"I never said it was safe," Theo said. Still so annoyingly calm. "I just said it was safer than above."

"Well, trapped down here with a bunch of fucking infected and nowhere to run doesn't *feel* much safer than above."

He looked back into the darkness. The screaming grew louder. The footsteps banging against the damp, mouldy, mossy brick pathway grew louder, too. Every now and then, she heard water splashing, the echo filling the tunnel even more.

"What the hell do we do?" Keira asked.

She held Nisha's hand even tighter. She kind of hoped the kid hadn't noticed. But she wasn't stupid. She looked around at Keira, and then at Theo, and at Rufus. And she could tell without hearing that something was going on. That something was happening.

"Because we need to do something fast," Keira shouted. "Very fucking fast."

Theo tried the door again. Booted it. An escape attempt that failed rather miserably.

And then he looked back around, into the dark, and he took a deep breath and sighed. "Only one choice."

"And what choice is that?"

He didn't speak.

"Theo," Keira said. "What choice is—"

"The water," he said.

"The water? No fucking way."

"If we jump in there, we can swim through the grate to the other side."

"You're seriously suggesting jumping into sewage?"

A series of cries echoed through the tunnel. They were getting closer.

"I don't see what other choice we have," he said.

She shook her head. Looked down into the murky darkness. It smelled so fucking bad. Like shit. Literally. Because that's what it was. A river of shit.

But it was so much worse than that. She couldn't see what was in the water—thankfully. But she didn't need to. She could use her imagination.

Piss.

Blood.

Vomit.

Semen.

The rotten waste from dead animals.

It was a cocktail of death. Jumping in there and swimming through it was a death sentence in itself.

But... Theo was right.

What other choice did they have?

"We should never have fucking followed you," Keira said.

She stood there. By the side of the water. When she looked over her shoulder now, she could see silhouettes in the darkness. Or were they in her imagination? She wasn't sure. She couldn't tell.

"It's now or never," Theo said.

"Why do you sound like you're enjoying this?"

He didn't answer. Which was kind of worrying.

She listened to the footsteps echoing louder.

She listened to the screams inching closer.

She closed her eyes and shook her head.

"Why am I considering this? Why the fuck am I considering this?"

She held Nisha's hand tight. Fuck. She didn't even have the time to tell her what she was doing. She didn't even have the time to warn her. She didn't even know if Nisha could fucking *swim*.

But she stood there. At the edge of the water. Looking down into its murky depths.

She took a deep breath of the putrid air, which made her gag, made her heave.

"Why are you doing this? Why are you doing this?"

And then she felt something heavy slam into her left side.

And before she could even brace herself...

She fell into the water.

She fell right in. The water submerged her. She felt it clawing up her nostrils like thick tar. And she felt it tickling the back of her throat like someone was slipping their hand down her neck, tightening, tightening, tightening...

She looked around, and all she could see was darkness.

She looked around, and all she could see was...

She could feel it.

That hand.

Clinging on to her arm.

Squeezing.

Squeezing so tight she could feel it digging into her skin, and —oh fuck, was it a bite? Was it a—

And then the hand loosened its grip, or the teeth, or whatever they were. And suddenly, she was free again.

Free of the grip.

She floated there in the water. She couldn't breathe. And she was—she was choking. She was choking and she was going to drown in a sea of shit and—

Air.

Air filled her lungs.

She gasped. Coughed. Almost choked and spluttered. She was breathing. She was breathing, and she was above the water. She was above the surface.

Only...

Only somehow, that made it worse.

Somehow, it made the smell even worse.

She could taste it, bitter on her lips.

And she could feel it stinging her eyes.

It made her want to throw up.

It made her want to puke.

It made her want to...

Screams.

Shrieks.

And a hand on her arm—

Theo.

"Come on," he said. "Through here."

She couldn't see him. She couldn't see where *here* was.

Her eyes were stinging.

The putrid taste of shit was making her heave.

And she could taste blood, too.

Blood.

That hand, holding her arm, squeezing tight.

An infected.

But where were they now?

"Now!" Theo said.

She looked around and saw Rufus splashing through the water like he was having the time of his life.

She looked around and saw the infected silhouettes racing down the tunnel.

She turned around and saw Theo right by the bars leading into the other side of the sewer.

And then...

Her stomach sank.

Her hand.

Her left hand.

There was nothing in her left hand.

No *one's* hand in her left hand.

"Nisha," she muttered.

She looked around in the water.

She looked around the sewer.

She looked all around.

But the more she looked... the more her stomach sank.

The more she looked... the more the reality sank in.

Nisha wasn't here.

Nisha wasn't here at all.

Nisha was gone.

NISHA

* * *

Nisha was floating in the darkness, and she realised she'd been here before.

This was where she was in the dream, where she couldn't see her body. Where she couldn't see *anything*. She couldn't see anything, and of course, she couldn't *hear* anything because she could *never* hear anything, could she?

But she could taste this awful taste in her mouth. Really bad. Like all the worst smells she'd ever smelled, turned into taste and poured down her throat.

She couldn't breathe. She felt like she had no body. She felt like she had no arms, no legs, no anything. She was just... floating.

Floating through nothing.

Floating in space.

And she didn't feel scared. She didn't feel anything at all. Not really. She just felt... calm. Like the more she fell into the darkness, the faster that happened, then the sooner she was going to see Dad again.

And that was what she wanted.

That was what she wanted more than anything.

She just wanted to see Dad again.

She tried to remember what'd happened to put her in this place. It was all very blurry. They were in the horrible sewer place, her, Keira, Rufus, and this man, Theo. And then she looked around, and she smelled the bad people and felt the bad people getting closer. And she saw Rufus barking and saw Keira shouting at the weird man, Theo.

And then the next thing she knew...

The sudden flash inside her.

And now darkness.

She realised then, as she floated, that she wasn't dreaming. And she did still have her body. She was in the water. She was in the nasty sewer water, where all the poo and wee and horrible stuff floated.

Only she couldn't swim.

She couldn't swim, and she was falling.

She was falling deeper into the water.

Deeper into the...

Cave.

She wasn't sure why she thought of the word "cave." 'Cause this wasn't a cave. She was in the water, and she was sinking deeper in the water, and...

Suddenly, she wasn't sinking.

She didn't feel like she was sinking at all.

She felt like she was floating.

Like she was floating on a sea of...

Bats.

She looked down, and she saw them all. Saw their little wings flying along, carrying her along. And even though they were bats, and she couldn't imagine what a sad bat looked like, something was sad-looking about them.

She looked down at them as they floated along. Looking so sad.

She looked down as they tried to hold her, as they tried to stop her falling further.

She looked down, and she fell further and further into the darkness, and...

It's not your time yet, dear.

That voice.

That voice in her head.

A whisper.

A whisper. But she was *hearing* it, she thought.

And she understood it right away.

And it was as clear as she'd ever heard anything.

And when she blinked and tried to shield her eyes from the horrible stinging in the darkness... she opened her eyes and saw someone.

Floating above her.

It was hard to explain what she was looking at. Because it was not like anything she'd ever seen before. She felt like she couldn't understand it. Like... it was more of a *feeling* than anything. A feeling. A warmth in her chest.

Bats.

But this thing was reaching for her in its own way.

It was reaching towards her.

Trying to lift her up.

Trying to...

We need you, dear.

We need you, Mother.

We need...

And suddenly, she understood.

Suddenly, it made sense.

It all made sense.

In a way she couldn't even understand properly in a normal way... it made sense to her.

Without you, we are weak.
Without you, we are nothing.
Without you, we are...
In danger.
Because she is stronger.
She is...

She tumbled further down into the darkness.

She tumbled further down into the sea of bats.

She stared up at the *FEELING,* and she felt their arms carrying her, cradling her, holding her.

We need you, Mother.
We need you to stay strong.
We need you to survive.
We need you to...

And then this thing. This feeling.

It changed.

It changed, and she saw...

Dad.

Dad looked down at her. He smiled at her like he always smiled at her. And he was standing in this hole. This hole of life.

Come on, angel, he signed. *You will be safe here.*

And even though she didn't know how to swim, suddenly she *did* know how to swim, and she was floating; floating down towards Dad, floating down towards the hole of light, floating down towards the place where she was safe, the place where she could be okay; where everything was going to be okay again.

She kept on going.

Kept on floating.

Kept on drifting.

Kept on sinking...

But she smiled.

Because she was going to be with Dad again soon.

Everything was going to be okay again soon.

She reached out her fingers.

Stretched out her shaking hand.

It's okay, angel, Dad signed. *I'm here. I'm...*

And then she felt something grab her back, and suddenly, it yanked her away from the tunnel of light, away from the safety, away from Dad, and back towards the bats, and the *FEELING*, and...

SARAH

* * *

The headlights hurtled down the road towards Sarah and Carly.

The infected raced through the trees towards them.

And all they could do was stand there.

Sarah's leg ached with pain. Carly stood beside her, holding onto her. She was suffering badly after her fall and after she'd rolled her ankle. Neither of them were in good shape. Neither of them were in good shape at all.

She stood in the middle of the dark country road.

Watched the headlights race closer.

Behind, the infected hurried through the trees.

Their screams filled the silent night.

And all Sarah could do was stand there.

All she could do was wait.

The woods behind her. Filled with infected.

The car. Or was it a van? Or something bigger? Hard to tell at the speed it was coming.

But fuck. That didn't matter.

All that mattered was that it was flying up the road.

And her leg and Carly's leg. Both knackered. Both absolutely knackered.

She stood there shaking.

She swallowed a lump in her throat.

She held her breath and closed her eyes, and...

No.

No, she wasn't giving up.

"Come on," she said.

She staggered across the road, clinging on to Carly. Carly winced with every step. And every step Sarah took was pretty fucking painful, too.

But she kept on going.

Because she had to.

She couldn't admit defeat.

She couldn't give up.

"I don't think—I don't think I can run much further."

And it didn't make total sense. Carly was supposed to be able to stop the infected. She was supposed to be able to hold them back.

And yet, right now, she seemed... weak.

She seemed broken.

She seemed exhausted.

Right when Sarah needed her to help the most.

And that matched up with what she'd told her.

Told her about only having so much energy.

Only having so much strength.

And the very fact the infected were here, too... that added up, too.

"Come on. We can do this."

She kept on walking across the road.

She kept on staggering across the street.

She kept on going. Focusing ahead. Only ahead.

She couldn't look back at the car.

She couldn't think about who it might be. Or what it might mean.

She just had to keep going.

And then...

Infected.

Right ahead.

Three of them.

Running past the trees and right towards them both.

Sarah stood there, then. Surrounded by infected on all sides. She needed Carly to do something now. She needed her to help her. Just as she'd helped her before already.

But at the same time... she didn't want Carly to do anything that might put herself in danger.

And not just because there were questions she still had.

Things she still didn't completely understand.

She looked around at Carly.

She saw she was crying, her face illuminating in the glow of the headlights.

Only...

Those tears.

They were tears of blood.

"I can't... I can't hold them back forever," Carly said. "They're... breaking through. They're getting stronger. They're..."

The infected ran across the street.

Ran towards Sarah.

Towards Carly.

At least thirty of them.

All surrounding them.

And that car still approaching...

Suddenly, Carly grabbed Sarah. She held her by the shoulders.

"You need to understand how it works. Before it's too late."

What, now?

Was now really the moment for...

And then Carly leaned into Sarah's ear and she told her.

She stepped away. And as the reality sunk in... her skin turned cold.

Because what she'd just told her.

What she'd just told her about why Nisha and The Girl were different.

What she'd just told her about what happened when *two* of them were in close proximity...

The *power* they had...

And then suddenly, she stroked Sarah's face as another tear of blood rolled down it.

"I know it's not easy to hear. I know it's a lot to digest. But I feel like you probably knew this already. I can see from the look in your eyes."

Her heart raced.

She couldn't think.

"I'll do what I can," Carly said. "Now you have to do your part."

And then she turned around, and she let her eyes roll back into her skull.

The infected kept on running.

Running as Carly stood there, shaking.

Racing towards her.

Running, as time ran out.

"Carly, no," Sarah said. "We need to go. We need to get away. We need to..."

And then, just like that, the infected...

Stopped.

It all happened in the space of a second.

But it was a second that felt like forever.

The infected.

All of them stopped.

All of them froze.

They all stood there and started shaking as the car continued to drive towards them.

And Carly...

Carly stood in the middle of them.

Shaking too.

Blood oozed down her cheeks.

Frothy saliva trickled from the corners of her lips.

And she was letting out this ghastly, possessed gasp as she stared right up into the sky, up into the darkness.

Blood spluttering from her nostrils, and her ears, and under her eyes, as her face grew more and more purple, and...

The infected.

Suddenly... they stopped.

They gasped.

And then, one by one, they started dropping.

Dropping to the ground.

And then wriggling and writhing around on the ground, as Carly stayed standing, as her shaking grew more violent, as more blood started spurting from her lips and her ears and her nostrils... and as her face went from purple to a greeny-bruised shade, as blood vessels burst across her face, and in her rolled back eyes, and...

The infected's heads burst.

One by one.

Bursting.

Popping.

Fireworks of blood splattering everywhere.

That horrible gasp still seeping from Carly's clenched teeth.

"The light," Carly muttered. "Not the dark. The light."

And the ramifications of what she'd told her, still replaying in her head, again and again and again.

She watched the infected's heads bursting, one by one.

She watched them shaking.

Screaming with pain.

Writhing around on the road.

And then, as the car ground to a halt, as the lights lit Carly up,

Sarah watched as Carly stumbled around and looked right back at her, her eyeballs completely red now.

And deep in the midst of her gasp... Sarah swore she heard her scream.

"GO!"

Men.

Climbing out of the car.

Running towards her.

Holding...

Rifles.

She went to turn around.

Went to run.

But before she could turn... she would never forget the last thing she saw.

Carly's head.

Exploding.

Blood splattering out of her broken, shattered skull.

Her body twitching and shaking like someone having a seizure.

And then falling limply to the ground with a thud.

Silence.

KEIRA

* * *

Keira floated atop the dark, murky water, her body filled with dread.

Because she couldn't see Nisha anywhere.

See was quite a bold term to start. She couldn't *see* much at all. The pitch-black abyss of the sewer water underneath her. A few silhouettes flickering at the side of the tunnel. Her eyes stung, all clogged up with horrid, nasty shit from below. She could hear the echoing cries of the infected, racing down the path beside the water. And she could hear splashing, too. Upstream.

She could hear Theo. Shouting at her. "Hurry up! Come on!"

But there was no trace of Nisha.

Her heart raced. Her body tensed up. Nisha. She was right here. She was holding her hand. And now... now, she was nowhere to be seen.

Which could only mean one thing.

The water.

She was somewhere under the water.

She looked down into that dark pit below. She swore she could see bubbles rising to the surface. And as much as she tried to calm herself, as much as she tried to steady herself, she couldn't help seeing Nisha sinking, descending, falling further and further below the water.

"You need to hurry!" Theo shouted.

She heard his voice. She looked up in his general direction. And as much as she desperately wanted to get the hell out of here right now... she couldn't leave Nisha behind.

"Go," she shouted.

"What? The infected. They're—"

"Go," Keira said. "Save yourself. I need to... I need to save her."

She looked down at the water, and she tried not to think about it again. She couldn't let herself think about any of it again.

So she held her breath, and she dunked her head under the water.

She hated being underwater. She'd always hated being underwater. She hated it as a kid. Did everything she could to avoid jumping into the deep end during swimming lessons back at school. When she was at the pool with her friends, she'd do everything she could to stop them from noticing that she didn't like being underwater, which was her least favourite thing.

But they always noticed.

The water was always there.

Waiting for her.

And it felt like everything had been building up to this very moment.

She squeezed her eyes shut. She couldn't let any more of that nasty shit in her eyes. Probably caught a tonne of diseases down here already.

But she couldn't keep her eyes closed for long. She *had* to open them. She had to look. She had to try and see.

But she didn't hold much hope of seeing.

Not down here.

She squeezed her eyes open. Squinted just a little.

Nothing but darkness.

Something solid sticking to the corner of her eye.

Clinging on.

She kept her lips sealed as tight as she could. She flailed around, hoping to catch a stray arm, leg, or anything.

Just anything.

A limb. That's all she needed.

She just needed to grab her.

And then drag her back to the surface.

And then, maybe then, everything would be okay.

She flailed around.

She tried to find her.

Tried to find just *some* sign of her.

She felt something nudge against the back of her hand. Something solid. Thought it might be her. Thought it might be Nisha.

But when she felt closer, she realised it wasn't a person at all. It felt more like an old tire. Flailing around, unsettled by the action.

She held her breath. Her heart raced. Her head grew tense. She couldn't hold on much longer.

But the second she came up for air... she knew it was an admission.

It was an acceptance.

An acceptance that she couldn't find Nisha.

And the next time she submerged, the next time she tried to find her... she knew the chances were even slimmer.

She stayed under the water for as long as she could. And then lights began flashing in her eyes, flickering across her vision. Her lungs began to tingle, began to ache. She kept on holding her breath. Kept on holding on.

She had to stay under here.

She had to find her.

She had to…

Instinctively, she floated up.

Up to the surface.

She gasped. Momentarily, it was a relief. She needed air so badly. So, so desperately.

But then the smell of the air filled her lungs, and the taste of the shitty water covered her lips, and the reality of her situation weighed down heavily on her shoulders.

Nisha.

She was under the water.

She was gone…

She floated around there. The shrieks were growing louder. More of them were splashing into the water. Tumbling in as they chased after her, pursued her. She couldn't hear Theo shouting anymore. Which probably meant he was gone.

And she couldn't blame him for leaving. He'd done the right thing for himself.

She had to stay here.

She had to stay here for Nisha.

She looked down at that murky water. She took a few deep breaths to try and calm her shaky limbs. She held her breath. Closed her stinging eyes.

"It's okay," she said. "I've got you. I'm coming for you. I'm…"

And then, suddenly, she noticed something when she opened her eyes.

It was only a split-second thing.

But a split second was all she really needed to understand.

Rufus.

Floating beside her.

Looking at her with these big, wide eyes.

Like… he understood.

He looked at her.

Tilted his head as he stared at her, crying, sobbing.

And then he looked down at the water, and something amazing happened.

Something truly remarkable happened.

Rufus dunked himself into the water and disappeared below the surface.

RUFUS

* * *

Rufus saw the sad look on Nice Lady's face and saw her doing the thing where the water came out of her eyes and mouth went all curved at the bottom and he could hear the noise coming out of her mouth and what she was saying and it was the name of the other one the one he didn't like the one who he used to like but who he didn't like as much lately he didn't like her as much because she reminded him of the nasty ones the ones who hurt Nice Lady who looked after him who made her bleed and he wanted to attack them he wanted to bite them but he was too scared he was too afraid because she ran at him after biting Karen and bit him on his back and he didn't know why 'cause he was just trying to be a good dog he even wagged his tail at her even though she made him feel scared even though she bit him and hurt him but that's how the girl the lady called "Nisha" made him feel now too.

But he could see the sad on the lady's face which was weird 'cause they were in water and Rufus loved water it was the best thing Karen used to take him out on long walks and whenever he saw water she'd shout at him to come back but he couldn't stop himself he'd just run towards that water and then he'd jump in it and splash around in it and Karen looked like she was mad at first but she wasn't because she was laughing and then they'd get home and she'd rub him with the towel and he'd bark and they'd laugh and they'd play and he missed her he missed her lots but the people now were nice too cause he was in the water again so they knew he liked water too.

But he could hear the nasty ones who bit running and he could hear them splashing in the water now and getting closer and he could see the way Nice Lady looked so sad and he could see her shaking her head and shouting "Nisha! Nisha!" and suddenly even though Rufus didn't like the Nisha he felt like he was out running through a park when Karen was throwing ball and he was running after ball and she said "fetch" and he'd run get it and bring it back and he wasn't sure but he thought the lady said "fetch" but maybe she didn't but it didn't matter because Rufus loved water so he flipped around and swum down into the dark water after the Nisha.

He wagged his tail and swum down into the dark and he loved the water he loved how cold it felt he loved how nice it felt and he didn't know why everyone was so scared and so sad because it was great down here and there were loads of great smells and tastes in this water too Mmm nice taste of animal dung his favourite oh and there's more Mmm nice all so nice all so—

No he was fetching the Nisha he couldn't taste nice things now even though he wanted to he didn't understand why Karen used to tell him off for eating the nice things on walks like the dead animals and the animal dung but she did and then she gave him nice treats when he dropped it so sometimes he picked it up just so she'd give him nice treats and she didn't know any better the silly Karen.

He swum further down in to the dark and he couldn't see the Nisha but even though he couldn't smell like normal down here he could *feel* that she was nearby and he just needed to keep going just needed to keep swimming further and further and if he kept swimming he'd find her he'd get her and then he'd bring her back like fetch and the lady would be happy and maybe she'd give him treats she'd let him swim forever she'd give him all the nice things.

And then he felt someone else nearby.

They were holding on to the thing at the back of him that he sometimes chased when he turned around and saw it moving and it surprised him.

And they were holding it tight really tight so tight it hurt.

He kicked and tried to break free because he couldn't swim if they were holding him and suddenly he felt weird he needed to get out the water he loved the water but he'd been in the water too long he'd...

Then the feeling went away and he was free free in the water free to swim free to fetch free to make Nice Lady happy free to...

Then he saw her the Nisha the one who he used to like but now didn't like cause she was like the bad who bit his Karen and when he saw her he was scared because he thought she might bite him or hurt him and he wanted to swim away.

But then he thought about the sad on Nice Lady's face and he thought about how she said "fetch" and he thought about how happy she'd be with him if he fetched her like a stick in the woods.

And he grabbed her with his mouth and he turned around and dragged her up up back up to the dark above.

Holding on to her.

Fetching her.

And then he saw the other bad.

The other bad getting closer.

Trying to reach him trying bite him trying to—

Keep swimming keep climbing keep—

The hand against him again.

Sharp feeling in his fur.

He held on to the Nisha with his mouth and he got closer to the top closer to the nice lady closer to...

The hand around his thing went tight again.

So tight that it made him yelp out.

And then something bad happened something bad something that meant he wouldn't get no treat something that made him bad dog.

He opened his mouth and the Nisha fell.

SARAH

* * *

Sarah ran.

She ran through the woods. Her leg hurt every time her right foot hit the ground. Sent a jolt of pain right the way up her leg, from her ankle, through her body. Her back ached. Like someone had a clamp around her lower spine and kept on tightening and tightening, squeezing and squeezing...

But she couldn't slow down. And she couldn't look over her shoulder.

She had to keep going.

The memory kept on replaying, flashing in her mind.

Carly.

Standing there in the road.

The infected.

Writhing around on the concrete beneath her.

Gasping.

Spluttering blood.

Carly's face growing more and more purple until...

That explosion.

The sound of her skull.

Cracking.

Splitting.

Bursting.

A shiver ran down her spine.

A bitter taste filled her mouth.

Carly.

She hadn't known her long. But in the time she had known her... she'd saved her life.

More than once.

And now she was gone.

And all Sarah had was the knowledge.

The knowledge of what Carly told her.

About the infected.

About Leonard.

About the power people like her had.

And about...

Nisha.

Sarah's heart thumped harder. The memory of Carly's final words replayed again and again.

The things she'd told her.

The knowledge she had.

She couldn't be right.

She couldn't possibly be telling the truth.

Could she?

But then she remembered what Carly did in her final moments.

She remembered the way her eyes rolled into the back of her skull.

The way she fell to her knees, tensing, shaking, foaming at the lips.

The way she'd made the infected all fall to the ground, and all burst, and...

And then she thought about the pain in her back. The pain

she told herself she'd always been battling with. The pain she tried to convince herself she'd always been struggling.

The denial that it was getting worse.

Far, far worse.

She shook her head. She had to etch that memory from her mind. She couldn't keep going there. She couldn't keep thinking about it.

She had to keep running.

She swore she could hear them somewhere in the distance. Approaching. The infected? Or the men from the military vehicle? She wasn't sure. She had no fucking clue. She didn't know where she was. She didn't know where the hell she was going in this pitch-black woods. She didn't know if she was getting closer to Keira, Nisha, and Rufus or further away from them. Fuck, she didn't even know if they were still alive or not.

But she kept on going.

She kept on running.

Limping away.

Because it was all she could do now.

She thought about Carly as her leg and back pain intensified. She thought about how short a space of time she'd known her. She'd rescued her. Saved her from the mass of infected. And then she'd come to Sarah's aid when she'd been caught up with those incel, XL Bully loving weirdos.

She'd helped her. Bandaged her.

And in the end, she'd died for her.

She tasted bitterness. She hadn't known Carly for long. But she felt like she'd known her for years. Like she was entirely comfortable in her presence.

She'd done everything she could to try and break Carly out of her self-inflicted isolation.

And now she was alone.

She staggered further through the woods when suddenly, the pain grew too strong, too intense.

She planted her hands on a tree in the darkness. She panted. She didn't want to stop. She didn't want to rest. It was too risky to take a break right now. Far too dangerous.

But the pain in her body had other ideas.

The pain that had crippled her all her life.

The pain that had defined her.

She tried to take another step into the darkness, deeper into the woods.

A bolt of agony shot right up her back.

She gulped.

And then she turned around, and she let herself slide down the tree until she hit the damp ground.

She sat there. Sat there in the silence of the woods. She stared up at the moon. She felt warm tears clawing down the sides of her face. She was crying. She was crying for Carly. Because Carly was a good woman. She was a good person. And she'd died protecting *her*.

And Sarah... never felt like she deserved anyone doing anything for her.

Let alone *dying* for her.

She thought about Harry.

Hands on her thighs.

She thought about Dean.

Breaking out of the flat.

And then she thought about Harry's screams.

And the jug of acid.

And...

She sat there in the darkness, and she swallowed a lump in her throat as the tears flowed down her face.

As the rain began to pour from above.

As it filled the silent darkness of the woods.

She sat there, and she thought of Harry.

She sat there and thought of how much she'd wanted him before he abused her.

And how, even *after* he'd abused her... she still wanted him.

She sat there and thought of Dean and how much she wanted him here right now, even after everything she'd been through at his hands.

Even after everything he'd suffered.

She sat there and wrapped her hands around her legs and buried her face between her thighs, and she thought of the strength she'd felt when she stood up to that incel fucker and his friends.

She thought about how she'd exorcised her demons.

And even so... she thought about how hopeless she still felt.

How *weak* she still felt.

She pressed her face harder against her legs, and as the rain poured down from above... Sarah cried.

KEIRA

* * *

It all happened so fast.

Rufus.

Disappearing into the water.

Deep into the depths of the sewer water, where Nisha must've submerged.

"Rufus!" Keira shouted. Even though the infected were running through the sewers towards them. Even though she could hear them tumbling into the water, splashing around, gargling and splattering. Could they swim? Why wouldn't they be able to swim? They weren't zombies. They were infected people. Infected. Enraged.

And if she didn't move fast, she was in deep shit.

She looked down at the water as her hair stuck to her face. Slimy shit oozed down her cheeks. Her heart raced fast. She could barely breathe—a combination of the adrenaline and the coldness of the water. The horror of the situation. Of the entire situation.

Nisha was gone.

Rufus was gone.

She looked up in the direction they'd come from, into the darkness.

She could still hear those echoey groans racing towards her.

She looked back around.

Into the darkness.

Then she looked over to her right, where Theo had disappeared.

He'd led her down here.

He'd led them all down here.

And now he was gone.

Now he was fucking gone.

She floated there in the water, and she didn't want to swim away. She couldn't swim away. Because without Nisha... what was the point of anything?

Without Rufus... what was left?

Was survival enough when there was nothing to survive for?

She went to submerge herself in the horrible water again when suddenly, a splash emerged right in front of her.

Rufus.

It was Rufus.

He was yelping.

Whining.

"Good boy," Keira said. In shock. Stroking his damp fur. He'd made it. He'd actually made it. "Good lad. Good... good boy. Good..."

And then she felt something nudge her ankle.

Something solid.

Something cold.

Something like...

A hand.

Nisha's hand?

She held her breath and submerged herself deep in the water.

She flailed around her ankle. Tried to find that hand—or whatever the hell it was—that just bumped into her ankle. She'd felt something. She'd definitely felt something. Had Rufus saved her? Fuck, she was going to give him all the treats in the world if he'd saved her.

But...

Was it already too late?

She'd been in the water for a long time now.

What if it was already too late?

She reached around her ankle. Searched. Kept on looking. She had to be down here. She had to be close. She had to be...

And then she felt it.

A hand.

A hand.

Wrapping around her wrist.

Only it wasn't Nisha's hand.

It was...

Another hand.

She tried to pull her hand away.

Tried to kick the infected in the water away.

She pushed her feet into its shoulders, and she pushed down hard as she felt the thrashing beneath her, getting stronger, getting more desperate...

And then she felt another hand.

Down there.

In the water.

Beside her.

Fingers.

Limp, cold fingers.

She held that hand.

She held that hand she recognised.

A hand she'd held before.

A hand she'd held so often.

She clenched it tight.

She held her breath.

And she pulled it up towards her with all her strength.

She saw her appear.

Saw her appear right in front of her.

It was dark.

It was cold.

But she could see her silhouette rising from the depths of the water.

Nisha.

"It's okay," Keira said, holding her, clenching her tight. "I've—I've got you. It's going to be okay, baby. I've got you."

She stroked her back as her heart raced. She paddled towards the opening where Theo had disappeared. The infected beneath her. She couldn't feel them. She couldn't feel them thrashing around anymore.

So she swam.

She swam with Nisha.

With Rufus wagging his tail and panting as he swam beside her.

"Good boy," she said to him. "Such a good boy."

She swam towards the metal railings and tried to squeeze through. She was going to have to let go of Nisha to get through. Fuck. She still hadn't made a sound. Her body was so limp.

She needed to get to the other side.

She needed to help Nisha.

She needed to get the water from her lungs.

She needed to...

She pushed against the railing.

She squeezed Nisha through.

Then she patted Rufus and urged him through.

"That's it. It's okay. Everything's... everything's gonna be okay."

She went to swim through the gap when suddenly she felt something.

She felt... a sense of immediate uncertainty. That was the only way to put it.

A sense of dread.

A pain.

A shooting pain.

Right across her left forearm.

A coldness.

Seeping through her bones.

Dripping down her spine.

An almost anti-climactic sense of inevitability about it.

But as Keira dragged her arm away and swam to the side of the sewer, her mind was only on Nisha.

"Come on," she said as she laid her down on the dirty, filthy floor. "You're going to be okay, my love. It's all going to be okay."

She pressed her hands against her chest in a way she'd done so many times in her career as a nurse.

"You're going to be okay…"

She pushed down on her chest.

Again.

And again.

Rhythmic motion.

That same rhythmic motion.

"I'm here, darling. I'm here."

And as Rufus sat by her side, wagging his tail, as the infected splashed around behind the grates in the water, and they banged at the door, trying to break through to this section of the sewer… Keira did everything she could to ignore the stinging pain.

The stinging pain on her left forearm.

The trickle of blood oozing down it.

"It'll be okay," she said, shaking, shivering. "Everything's going to be okay…"

SARAH
---

* * *

When the sun rose, Sarah opened her eyes.

It was bright. Really bright. Shining between the trees, making her squint. She wanted to close her eyes. She wanted to fall back to sleep. She wanted the darkness to surround her once more. Because at least she didn't have to suffer in the darkness. At least in the darkness, she could forget. Forget what she'd been through her whole life. Forget what she'd seen. Forget what she'd lost.

She blinked a few times. Rubbed her crusty eyes with her shaking fists. Her mouth felt dry and furry. A bitter, slightly acidic taste clung to the back of her throat. She could smell something. A combination of sweat and piss. Probably her own.

And a slight metallic hint, too.

Blood.

She looked around. Saw trees. The leaves gently shaking in the breeze. Sweat trickled down her face and lips, adding to the nasty tang. Her heart pounded. Nausea gripped her stomach tight. Shit. She'd actually managed to sleep last night. Somehow, she'd dozed off in the middle of the woods. Dangerous. She might've got herself bitten. Got herself killed.

But she didn't feel any pain. Or at least any *new* pain. She always felt *some* sort of pain. Shooting pains shot down her spine, right down to her toes. That burning pain clawed across her right ankle, where that bastard dog bit her however the fuck long ago that was. Felt like only hours ago. But at the same time, it felt like forever ago.

She leaned back against the tree. The bright sunlight burned against her, making her sweat. She closed her heavy eyelids. She wanted to doze off again. She wanted to disappear into the darkness again.

But this time... she saw flashes.
Flashes of Carly.
Standing there.
Shaking.
Blood oozing from her nostrils, all over her face.
Biting her lip so hard it bled.
Digging her fingernails into her palms.
The infected.
All around her.
Lying down.
Shaking.
And then...
That sound.
That bursting sound.
The fireworks of blood and bone bursting all over the street.
She opened her eyes again.

She was exhausted. Weak. Her mouth felt so dry, and it hurt to swallow. She knew she should eat, but she wasn't hungry. Wouldn't be the first time in her life she'd chosen not to eat when she was hungry. Whenever she was stressed, the same pattern repeated. Gradually cutting down her portions of food until... nothing.

Surviving on water.

Wanting to eat. Wanting so desperately to eat.

But the mere thought of eating filling her with repulsion.

With dread.

Until she snapped out of it with an almighty binge the second she was feeling something like okay again.

She wasn't going to have the luxury of a feast anymore.

She sat there. Leaned back against the hard bark of the tree. Her back ached so badly. A small part of her wondered if it would've been such a bad thing if she were bitten in her sleep. If she were torn apart. At least if it happened in her sleep, she wouldn't even have the time to panic about it all that much.

But then a knot tightened in her stomach.

Nisha.

What Carly told her about Nisha.

And why she needed to stop her from reaching Leonard's place as a matter of urgency—if that was indeed where Nisha was headed.

And then...

She remembered those words.

Those final words Carly whispered to her before running into the middle of the road to hold back the infected.

The words that made her lower back ache, more and more.

The words that brought back memories of the hospital. The uncertainty. The denial.

She'd thought about those words repeatedly. She'd tried to convince herself that maybe she'd misheard. Maybe she was wrong. It was a tense moment. Incredibly heated. Maybe she'd misheard her in the frenzy.

But she realised how ridiculous that was. It didn't matter how much she tried to convince herself that maybe she was wrong... she knew what she'd heard. Exactly what she'd heard.

But she still couldn't quite comprehend the implications of those words.

She still couldn't fully understand how Carly knew what she knew.

But she knew one thing.

She'd seen what Carly did.

She'd seen how the infected fell around her.

How they *died* around her.

And she'd seen how that power had grown too strong for her.

She tasted that bitterness in her mouth again, so strong, so intense.

Her heart started pounding.

And then she turned around and vomited on the ground beside her.

The moment that bitter, hot vomit left her lips, she felt... lighter, somehow. Like a weight lifting from her shoulders. Her heart pounded. Sweat oozed down her face. Her chest felt tight, and her breathing wasn't easy. But she felt... *lighter*.

And as she lay there, she realised... she realised that in her mind, she wasn't lying on the ground with Harry's hands sliding up and down her thighs.

In her mind, she wasn't locked behind that door in Dean's cupboard.

She was standing in front of the wall.

And Dean's cupboard doors were open.

She lay there. And even despite all the loss, even despite all the pain, even despite all the trauma... she was still standing.

She was still standing. In a lot of fucking pain. And finding her ankle very fucking difficult to stand on.

But still standing.

And as long as she was still standing... she still had a chance.

She had a chance to go and search for Nisha.

She had a chance to find her.

And it was a chance she was going to take.

A chance she *had* to take.

She took a deep breath. Wiped vomit from her mouth. She

stood up, even though she was shaky, even though she was in pain. And then she looked out at the burning sun, shining brightly through the trees.

She took another deep breath.

She swallowed a vomity lump. Then spat a chunk of something out onto the ground.

And then she looked back up at that sunshine.

It was time to find Nisha.

It was time to find Keira.

It was time to do exactly what she had to do.

NISHA

* * *

Nisha was in a dark cave.

She couldn't see anything. It was darker than dark. Like, darker than the darkest night, when she was hiding from the monsters in the dark and had the quilt cover pulled over her face, and her eyes squeezed so tight that she couldn't see anything, she couldn't see anything at all, even if there *was* someone bad out there.

But this... this was different.

Total darkness. As dark as it must be for a blind person. No sounds, either. Deaf and blind. She turned her head, but nothing changed. She wasn't sure if she even *had* a head or was just floating.

Floating in the darkness.

Floating without a body.

But she could *feel* something...

It was kind of like when she was going to do something she was excited and scared about. When she was climbing a rollercoaster, Dad by her side, the wind against her face, the smell of donuts in the air, and the sugary taste of candy floss on her lips.

It felt like that. Right in the middle of where her belly was.

It felt like...

Power.

She looked down. She couldn't see anything. Just... darkness.

But she could *feel* something there. And even though it was a bit like the feeling she got when she was on the rollercoaster or when she was leaving school for the weekend... even though it felt a *bit* like excitement and also like *fear*... it was something completely different.

A feeling she had never felt before.

Something new.

Which was weird. 'Cause even though Nisha didn't really understand it, she thought every feeling was either excitement or fear at some level. And maybe even sadness a bit, too.

This was something different.

This was something new.

Suddenly, she felt something. She felt this air whooshing against her face. She felt these... *things* hitting her as they flew into her. She felt them, so many of them, hitting her. Banging into her. Headbutting her. They felt like stones.

But then... suddenly, even though she couldn't see... Nisha knew what they were.

They were bats.

She hung there in the darkness while the bats flew into her, and she didn't feel scared. She didn't feel scared at all. In a way, she felt... comfortable. She felt safe. Like she was lying in bed and under the covers, and everything was okay, everything was going to be okay.

She let more and more of the bats fly right into her when suddenly light filled her eyes.

She squeezed her eyes shut. 'Cause it was so bright. So bright it burned her eyes and made her feel sick and dizzy. Why was it so bright? It was brighter than anything she'd ever seen before. It kind of felt like she was right next to the sun, and it was shining right into her eyes, burning her, and that it was going to swallow her up and burn her and...

And then she saw something else.

Right in the middle of that burning light. She could see something else.

Something... dark.

Something... again, *different*.

Something she couldn't explain.

She looked at it and even though she didn't know what it was and even though she didn't know how to explain it 'cause it was different to anything else she'd ever seen before—in the same way that *feeling* was different to anything else she'd ever felt before—she didn't feel scared of it.

And she knew what it was.

Somehow, she knew what it was.

It *was* the feeling.

She could see it. This darkness. Like a dark circle in the middle of the light. And she knew if she reached out and touched it... something would happen. Something *big* would happen.

She stretched out her fingers. But she could feel something pulling her back. Something trying to stop her.

Yes yes that's it reach out Mother reach out you're strong enough now you're strong enough you're...

And seeing those words in her head, moving across the darkness like words on a screen, she wasn't sure what to think. Because she didn't like what that voice told her to do. She didn't like the things it tried to make her do.

But...

Reach out join us join us all join join join...

She felt the desperation in those words that she could somehow understand.

She squeezed her eyes shut, even though it was so hard to fight back, even though it was so hard to resist.

You're ready join us join us join us join...

And then she felt this bang in her chest.

Like her heart exploding.

She felt this scratching in her ears.

And all behind her eyes.

And then the lights turned red, and the bats all started flying hard at her and biting and filling up her mouth and her lungs and she couldn't breathe and she needed to cough to get them out to get them out to get them—

She coughed.

She spluttered a load of... of water everywhere.

And suddenly, she was in a different darkness. A *lighter* darkness, even though it was still really dark.

She was lying on a damp floor. It was dark all around. She was wet through. She could see someone right above her. It took her a few seconds to realise who it was.

But when she blinked away the nasty, smelly water a few times, she realised who it was.

Exactly who it was.

Keira.

She lay there. On the ground. And suddenly, it came back to her. Suddenly, she remembered.

The water.

Falling in the water. And losing her grip on Keira's hand. And sinking, sinking, and...

And she was okay.

She was coughing, but she was okay.

Even though she felt... tired. Like she couldn't keep the bad people away again. 'Cause it was too hard. And something bad would happen to her if she tried to keep them away again.

She coughed up all the water and all the nasty tastes and all the sick, and then she looked around. She saw that man standing there. The one she didn't like so much called Theo. He was holding a little lighter, which, even though it was little, lit up the darkness a lot.

Then she saw Rufus wagging his tail.

She looked back at Keira and even though she felt awful, she went to smile at her, when suddenly, she saw something on Keira's arm.

The second she saw it, her skin went cold.

Her body went numb.

Everything went cold.

Because in the darkness… Nisha could see something different about Keira.

Something on her arm.

Something bleeding.

A bite mark.

KEIRA

* * *

Nisha woke up.
She leaned forward, and she spluttered water everywhere. She coughed that water up. Choked it all over the sewer floor. And even though Keira could hear the infected cries echoing through the tunnel, even though she could smell the shit and the vomit and the rot of the sewer, and even though she could taste it at the back of her throat, making her heave... she didn't care.

Because Nisha was awake.

Nisha was alive.

Even the splitting pain on her left forearm drifted to the back of her mind.

The throbbing, burning pain she was trying to hide from.

The pain she was trying to deny.

"You're okay," she said as she held on to Nisha in the darkness. Stroking her damp hair. "I'm here. You're... you're okay."

And then she saw Nisha's gaze drift to her arm.

She saw her eyes widen.

And the reality hit her.

Hard.

Her heart raced. Her chest tightened. She didn't want to look at her arm. Because looking at her arm was accepting it. Looking at her arm was making it real.

But she couldn't hide from the truth for long.

She looked down at her arm, and she saw the blood.

She saw the toothmarks.

The bite.

No. Maybe it wasn't a bite. Maybe she'd just scratched her arm. Maybe she'd just caught it on a sharp piece of metal while she was dragging herself through that narrow gap. Or maybe it was a piece of debris that'd caught her. That was a possibility, wasn't it? That had to be a possibility, right?

But... no. As much as she tried to convince herself otherwise, and as much as she tried to convince herself that this was anything *but* a bite... she couldn't. She just couldn't.

And that made her dangerous.

That made her a threat.

"I don't mean to interrupt," Theo's voice said, breaking through the haze. "But we really could do with getting ourselves out of here as soon as possible. The infected aren't gonna wait for us to leave."

But Keira barely even registered his words. They drifted by her. She felt Rufus nudging his head against her leg. Whining a little as filthy water oozed down his fur.

All she saw was Nisha.

Lying there.

Staring up at her.

Pale.

All she saw were the tears in her eyes.

And those tears... they just made things even worse.

Because seeing those tears in her eyes was confirmation.

Confirmation of the truth.

Confirmation of the bite.

And she wasn't... she wasn't sad for *herself*, per se. She wasn't sad for herself at all.

She was sad because it meant she wouldn't be able to get Nisha away from here.

Because she wasn't safe with Nisha.

"Seriously," Theo said. "We don't have long left."

And his voice. It sounded like it was getting further away. Further down the tunnel. Maybe this was it. Maybe this was where things ended for their brief friendship—if it could even be called a friendship.

Down here in the sewers.

Down here in the sewers with Nisha.

Only...

Keira took Nisha's hands in hers. Held them. Tight.

"You need to go," she muttered.

Nisha shook her head. She thought maybe she wouldn't understand her, maybe she'd fail to hear her. But she clearly saw what she said. Read her lips.

And here she was, shaking her head. Tears rolling down her face.

"I'm sorry," Keira said, shaking her head. "But you're not safe with me now. Nobody is safe with me. You need to get out of here. You need to go. You need to..."

Suddenly Keira heard something.

An infected. Snarling. So close.

Right behind her.

And more of them.

Splashing around in the water.

"We need to go!" Theo shouted. "Now!"

Keira didn't even think. Not anymore.

She couldn't.

Nisha was too weak to hold back the infected. That much was clear.

So she grabbed Nisha.

She lifted her into her arms.

And as the infected raced through the darkness towards her, towards Rufus, she followed Theo, and she ran.

She ran. As fast as she could. Down the dark corridor. Clinging on to Nisha. Holding on to her. Even though she felt weak. Even though she felt dizzy. And even though she felt the pain creeping up her arm, into her shoulder, into her chest, filling her with that cold void inside... she kept on going.

"It's okay," she whispered. Even though Nisha couldn't hear her. "It's going to be okay."

She kept on running.

Kept on going.

She held her breath as her heart raced and her chest tightened, and she swallowed a lump of vomit in her throat, and she kept on going.

Running down the dark, slippery pathway beside the water.

Further and further into the darkness.

The snarls of the infected echoing closer behind.

She kept on going when suddenly she heard something up ahead.

Theo.

"Up here!" he said.

And she didn't know what he was talking about. Not at first.

Not until she looked up.

Saw him. Above her. Light shining down.

He was up a ladder.

A way out of here.

A way out.

She looked over her shoulder.

Saw the silhouettes shuffling closer.

Racing towards her.

She looked around at Rufus. "Get Rufus," she said.

"What?" Theo shouted.

"Help Rufus up," she said. "Right fucking now."

She heard Theo cursing under his breath. Saw him scrambling down the ladder.

And as she watched him lift Rufus, as she watched him take that whining, yelping dog up the ladder... she stood in front of Nisha, and she held her hand.

Nisha looked into her eyes, tears rolling down her cheeks. Shaking her head. She was moving her mouth. But no sounds were coming out. Or... small noises. Right from the pit of her throat. Pitiful noises.

Like she was trying to say "please."

Keira leaned towards her.

She kissed her on the forehead.

And then she stroked her hair out of her face and wiped a tear from her cheek.

You're going to be okay, she signed. Just like Nisha had taught her. *You're strong. Now go.*

She heard the infected inching closer.

She saw Nisha shaking her head.

Saw her crying.

And she felt that throbbing pain in her arm getting stronger and stronger and...

She knew what needed to happen.

She knew what Nisha needed to do.

She knew she needed to get away.

And as those screams echoed closer towards her... she waited for Nisha to let go of her hand.

"Go," Keira said. "Go."

Nisha shook her head.

"For me. Go. Now."

Nisha closed her crying eyes.

She shook her head.

And then she went to pull her shaking hands away.

And Keira braced herself.

She braced herself to do what she had to do.
Whatever she had to do.
Nisha was weak.
Nisha couldn't keep them away like she used to.
So she had to brace herself.
But then...
Something happened.
Nisha.
She pulled her hands away.
For just a second.
But then she tightened her grip on Keira's hands.
Hard.
Harder than Keira thought was possible.
"What..."
And then Nisha's neck cracked back.
Her eyes rolled back into her skull.
And blood started oozing down her nostrils.
Something was happening.

NISHA

* * *

Nisha held Keira's hands. She saw the bite on her arm, and she didn't want to run away from her. She didn't want to leave her.

She wanted to help her.

But she could smell the bad people coming.

She could *feel* them coming.

She could feel them getting closer and closer.

And as she stood there by the ladder, she didn't feel strong enough to stop the bad people. Not this time. Not anymore. She felt like if she *tried* to stop the bad people, then something really bad would happen to her. Something terrible. And she didn't want something terrible to happen to her.

But also, she didn't want anything terrible to happen to Keira.

But her arm.

The toothmarks on her arm.

No.

No, Keira couldn't die, too. She didn't want to be on her own with this weird man. And Rufus didn't like her. Rufus didn't like her, and she didn't know how to look after him properly, and he'd end up running away, and she'd lose him, just like she lost Kat...

She held Keira's hands. She watched her mouth moving. She could tell what she was trying to tell her. She could read her lips.

But she didn't even have to read her lips really. She could see from the look on her face what she was trying to say to her. What she was trying to tell her.

She was trying to tell her to go.

But Nisha didn't want to go.

Because she was scared to go.

She didn't want to go because she was scared to be on her own.

She didn't want to go because—

Let us take her dear let us take her almost ours almost ours and—

We get strong which means—

YOU get stronger...

All these noises in her head. Like bats. Flying around her head.

And getting louder, and louder, and louder.

Noises.

Noises she could hear.

Noises she could understand.

She gripped Keira's hand as she felt tears rolling down her cheeks and touching her lips.

She tasted the salt of the tears.

She stood there, and she wanted to tell Keira they had to get away. She wanted to tell Keira they had to run.

The bad people.

Getting closer.

Keira.

Standing right there.

Go, Keira said, her mouth moving. *Go...*

She went to let go of her hands.

She went to run away.

She was about to run when suddenly...

It all happened so fast.

She saw it.

Saw that dark circle in her head again.

The dark black circle in the light.

And she reached in towards it, and she fell in towards it, and suddenly she was falling, suddenly she was sliding down a big slide, and her belly was tickling, and wind was blowing against her face, and she was getting faster, and faster, and...

And suddenly she could see all the bad people.

Flying past her like bats.

Only...

No.

She was the bat.

She was the bat, and she was flying past *them*.

And then she saw more of them, and the more of them she saw, the stronger she felt. And then she realised she was seeing other people, too. Only they didn't look bad. They looked... normal.

They looked normal.

And she could feel herself getting *inside* them.

Just like she'd got inside the man inside the bunker.

Just like she'd got inside *all* those people inside the bunker.

Just like she'd...

Turned them.

Turned them bad.

And that's when she realised.

That's when it made sense.

That's when it all made sense.

The voice.

The feeling.

Everything.

Yes Mother you are Mother we serve you we get stronger when you get stronger.

Don't resist it don't fight it.
Let it get stronger let it happen let us...
Feed.

And she wanted to fall into it.

She wanted to disappear into it.

She wanted to *bathe* in it.

But the next thing she knew...

She was inside Keira.

And Keira felt... she felt different.

She felt like she was changing.

Turning *bad.*

That's it we're there now we have her now, dear, we have her and all will be okay, everything will be...

But then Nisha did something else.

That light.

The bright light all around her that she couldn't even explain.

She reached out for that light.

No don't no not strong enough not strong DON'T

And the more she saw these words in her head, the harder she stretched.

NO NO NO NO NO

She felt her fingers touch the light even though it felt like she was pushing two magnets against each other, and the closer she got to touching the light, the harder it pushed back.

And the stronger the words got.

NO NO DEAR NO DON'T MOTHER NOT STRONG ENOUGH TOO WEAK TOO...

And then she held her breath, and she touched the light.

And when she touched the light...

She felt the coldness inside Keira.

She felt it spreading up her arm, and through her body, through her veins.

She felt the bats. Flapping their wings.

But then she felt something else.

The light.
The warm light.
Warm light filling the cave.
She felt that light.
So strong inside her.
She felt that light swelling.
She felt it filling up her body.
Filling Keira's body.
And then she felt it bursting.
She felt the light exploding inside her and inside Keira.
She felt the coldness and the bats flapping away, turning around.
She felt the warmth.
And she saw The Girl in her head.
Smiling at her.
You did it, she said.
And then The Girl disappeared, the light surrounded her, and the warmth filled her body, and everything went...
Light.

KEIRA

* * *

It all happened in a flash.

Like, a literal fucking flash.

One moment, she was holding Nisha's hand. She could feel Nisha pulling her fingers away as they stood by that ladder. And Keira needed Nisha to run away. She needed her to run the hell away. 'Cause a bunch of infected were heading right their way, and if they weren't fucking fast, they were all gonna get caught up in them.

Rufus was above ground with that Theo guy, who she hadn't heard anything from for a while. But her and Nisha were still down here. Down here, surrounded by the stench of shit in the sewers. Down here, as the infected's screams and shouts and cries grew louder.

Down here, waiting for the goddamned end.

Only...

Nisha stopped moving away.

Her neck snapped back.

Blood oozed from her nostrils.

And for a moment, for just a moment, Keira felt that familiar sense of fear.

'Cause this didn't look good.

Nisha wasn't strong enough to hold them back anymore.

She opened her mouth to say her name, even though she knew it was pointless.

She went to take a step towards her.

And then she felt it.

A surge.

A surge of energy through her body, from her toes to her head.

That was the only fucking way she could describe it. A surge of... yeah. Energy. Vague as it sounded.

She felt her body shaking. Shaking with this intense cold.

She couldn't see a thing. And it wasn't like normal darkness, either. It wasn't like the darkness of the sewers. And it wasn't like she was somewhere bright and the lights had just been switched off.

It was... something else.

Pure darkness.

She felt this coldness inside her. And she realised where exactly it was. It was spreading up her arm. Spreading up from her *bite*.

She felt it hurtling through her system. Rapidly. And she realised what this was. She realised what this must be. This was it. This was the end. This was her turning into one of the infected. And she'd been too late to save Nisha. Nisha was in danger. Nisha was...

And then, suddenly, she felt something else.

Some things in life are impossible to explain. Like, truly impossible. Very few moments like that. Moments where the experience itself *speaks* for itself.

Not to jump to conclusions too prematurely.

But this felt like one of those moments.

She could see someone in front of her. Only faintly. But there was this... presence.

There was this...

Light.

And it felt like the light was seeping in through her fingers.

It felt like the light was entering the palms of her hands.

Climbing up her body.

It felt like it was searching for that bite wound.

It felt like it was climbing towards all the coldness creeping from that bite wound.

The darkness seeping from that bite wound.

And it felt like it was...

Fighting it.

And as she stood there in this darkness, right then, she understood.

The person in front of her.

The *presence* in front of her.

It was Nisha.

She stood there. Stood there in this darkness, holding Nisha's hand.

And as her body grew warmer, as the coldness in her arm grew less and less prominent... she understood.

Might sound crazy. Bear fucking with her. She *knew* how it sounded. It even sounded crazy to her.

But... there was just this knowledge.

This deep understanding.

This understanding of what was happening.

Of exactly what was happening.

She stood there, and she let the light fill the darkness.

She stood there, and she let the warmth fill the cold.

She stood there, and she held Nisha's hand, and she felt her body fill with light, and the pain leave her arm, and...

And then she was back.

She fell down. Clutched her chest, which ached like mad.

Nisha.

Nisha stood in front of her. Nose bleeding. Face pale. Ears bleeding a little, too.

But standing there.

Standing there in the darkness of this sewer.

The light shining down from the opening above.

And the infected cries creeping closer towards both of them.

She looked at Nisha. And Nisha looked back at her. Wide-eyed. Teary-eyed. Bloody-eyed, too.

But she looked back at her, then down at her bitten arm, then back up at Nisha, and... and she understood.

She just understood.

"Come on," she said. Then she signed it for luck.

She nudged Nisha up the ladder.

And then she clambered up it herself.

Up, out of the sewers.

Away from the infected.

And towards the light.

And as Keira climbed that ladder... she couldn't feel anything but amazement.

Because Nisha.

Nisha was far, far more powerful than she'd ever imagined.

SARAH

* * *

Sarah had no idea how long she'd been walking through the woods when she finally saw her first sign that the military was close.

It was a military vehicle. Abandoned by the looks of things. Nobody around. No weapons around. Nothing like that. There was a red patch on the side of it. Rust or blood? She wasn't too sure. Even when she scraped her finger against it and tasted it, it didn't answer any questions. Rust and blood tasted remarkably similar, didn't they?

She looked around the road. It was a fairly rural road. Tall trees and hedges on either side of her. A few birds flying overhead. A few crows calling. And the sun, beating down stronger than it'd beat down in days. The smell of the rain that'd fallen over recent days clawing its way into her nostrils, so strong, so bitter.

And so misleading, too.

Because she knew what *else* smelled like fallen rain on a warm day.

And she was eager not to run into *those* right now.

Very eager indeed.

She searched the military vehicle for some trace of life. But she couldn't find a thing. Her heart raced. If this were something to do with Leonard's group... then maybe it would lead her right to his place.

And if it led her right to his place... maybe it would lead her right to Nisha, Keira, and Rufus, too.

But what if she were wrong? What if this wasn't anything to do with Leonard's group? Or what if Keira and Nisha hadn't gone to Leonard's place themselves? There were bound to be other military groups out there, after all. Sarah had seen traces of a bunch of them along the way.

She had no idea whether she was heading in the right direction when it came to Nisha. And at the end of the day... admit or deny it all she liked; *she* was the most important person right now.

She stood there by the side of this military vehicle, on this silent road, when suddenly something caught her eye.

It was lying on the road by the side of the military vehicle. It looked like it'd been stamped on, a few footprints over the top of it. And it was sodden from the puddles on the ground, too.

But Sarah reached down for it. Picked it up.

And when she opened it, she found something she certainly didn't expect.

It was a leaflet. Some kind of map. Old, by the looks of things. An old map of Lancashire.

And on this map, as much as it was torn and tattered... she could see a faint line.

A faint line leading from a barracks near Wigan to...

The North Lancashire Barracks.

And bang in the middle of that route?

Preston.

A bitter taste filled Sarah's mouth. What did this mean? It looked like another group was trying to reach the North

Lancashire Barracks. Carly had mentioned that place. That was where Leonard was based. She hadn't known where exactly that barracks was located before now. But now...

It was right here in front of her.

And the way the faint line on the page cut right through the middle of Preston... could this be the group Sarah and Keira ran into when they were down that bridlepath, what felt like forever ago?

Or was it just a coincidence?

She stood there. Heart racing. Hands shaking.

She wasn't sure, really. She didn't know what to expect. Didn't have a clue. She didn't know whether this was just a coincidence, or whether it was a sign, or whatever.

But she knew one thing for sure.

It was another sign of the magnetic allure of the North Lancashire Barracks.

Of Leonard's home.

The mysterious Leonard.

She stood there. Stared down the road, right off into the distance. If other military groups were trying to reach this place, then if Keira and Nisha had been saved by a military group, *that's* where they would be going, too.

She knew she had to be careful. She knew she couldn't be complacent. She knew there was every chance that she was wrong. There was a whole host of everything that could go wrong. She knew that better than anyone. Her entire life felt like one tumbling domino after the next. So she certainly was not naive to life's complexities and its ever-growing ability to pull the rug from under one's feet when least expecting it.

But at the same time... Sarah knew with a growing certainty that she could head in only one direction.

She thought about Carly.

What she'd told her.

About Nisha.

And the power Leonard would have if he got his hands on Nisha...

She took a deep breath.

Swallowed a lump in her dry throat.

Carly's words.

They were enough.

They were more than enough.

She gritted her teeth and buried her fingernails into her palms, and then she took a step.

And that's when she heard it.

It started with just a gentle rumbling somewhere in the distance.

Somewhere *behind* her.

And then it grew.

It grew to the point that she could *feel* the ground shaking somewhat.

She stood there. Felt her jaw clench. She'd heard that sound before, just once.

She'd felt that sensation before, too.

She didn't want to turn around.

She didn't want to look over her shoulder.

She didn't want to face the truth.

But as she stood there, as the sound grew in intensity... Sarah knew she didn't have a choice.

She turned around.

Slowly.

And then she saw it.

Right in the distance.

Her mouth went dry.

Her stomach turned.

And suddenly, Sarah knew she needed to get a long way away from here.

Fast.

KEIRA

* * *

Keira was bitten.

But somehow, she *knew* she wasn't infected.

She felt Nisha's cold, shaking hand gripping hers tightly. Her legs ached with every step she took. Her feet were sore. She couldn't stop shivering. Couldn't stop shaking. She felt tired. Exhausted. If she stopped, she might just fall asleep in an instant.

But it was developing into a gorgeous day. The dawn sun beamed down strongly from above. She felt its warmth, and it took the edge off the dampness a bit.

She felt like shit, sure. Her arm throbbed like mad. She'd been bitten. She'd actually been bitten.

But... she wasn't infected.

And she knew it. Deep inside her. She wasn't even sure *how* she knew. But she knew.

It wasn't denial.

Nisha had done something.

Which meant she was capable of far more than even Keira

first thought.

She looked at the abandoned street around her. At the cars long ago abandoned. Such a familiar sight now. She didn't like the silence. It was eerie. She kept thinking she saw movement behind the cracked windows of the terraced houses beside her. Dangerous place to be, a street like this. The rows of terraces didn't leave much room for her to escape if she needed to run suddenly. There was a really ominous atmosphere looming. She hadn't seen many infected outside the sewers. Many at all.

It felt like everything was just building up to something. To a moment.

A moment that she wasn't sure she wanted to face any time soon.

She couldn't smell the earthiness in the air. That's what she always checked for. There was no trace of the stench of the infected right now, either. Weird.

She watched Theo walk down the road up ahead. He kept glancing over his shoulder now and then, looking right at her. Then, turning around again. Shaking his head.

Theo was an... interesting character, to say the least. When she'd first run into him, he seemed incredibly reluctant to help her, Nisha, and Rufus.

But then he'd almost died in the sewers with them. And they'd been out of the sewers a good hour now—at least—and he was still walking with them.

And there was still something about him.

Something she couldn't quite place.

Something... familiar.

She smelled the slight hint of shit emanating from her soggy body. She felt her arm stinging where she'd been bitten. The sewer water and an open wound. That couldn't be a good combo. Had Theo noticed? He must've noticed. Maybe he'd put two and two together, too. He'd seen she hadn't turned. And he realised there was something special about that.

But maybe he hadn't noticed. In a way, whatever the status quo was... she kind of wanted it to stay that way. It was working for her right now.

And then she looked down at Nisha.

Nisha looked up at her with wide eyes and a pale face. She hadn't communicated with her since the sewer. Since that crazy, inexplicable moment, down there in the darkness. She seemed okay in herself. Considering she'd submerged in the sewer water. Considering she'd almost drowned. She was weak. But she was okay.

And there was another part of that entire crazy exchange that Keira couldn't forget.

The bite.

The infected. Sinking its teeth into her skin.

Trying to urge Nisha to flee.

Reaching the ladder.

Reaching that hatch.

And then...

Keira couldn't remember the exact sequence of events. She couldn't quite place how it all unfolded. Kind of like trying to remember a dream. There were fragments of it she could remember. Fragments of it—the burning light, the searing warmth.

But the more she tried to get hold of it... the more it slipped between her fingers.

Other than a burning knowledge.

An overwhelming confidence.

She was bitten.

But she wasn't infected.

She looked down at Nisha. At how pale she looked. How exhausted she looked. And she wondered if she was just in denial. That was a perfectly natural response to a death sentence, wasn't it? And Keira couldn't think of a more certain death sentence than a bite wound.

But... No.

Something had happened down there in the sewers.

Something had happened when Nisha took her hands.

Something had happened.

She knew Nisha could resist the infected. She knew she could resist turning. And she'd seen other things, too. She'd seen signs that Nisha might be able to *direct* the infected somehow.

But was the impossible, in fact, possible?

Could Nisha... *stop* the infection from taking hold?

It seemed far-fetched. It seemed crazy.

But this little girl had more abilities than Keira could even pretend to understand. And really, nobody knew *anything* about the infection, how it worked, or how it progressed. It certainly *seemed* unlike anything Keira had ever come across.

All Keira knew was that she had this confidence that, somehow, Nisha had stopped her bite mark turning her into a monstrous infected.

She looked around at the street. At all the debris. At all the abandoned cars. The smashed windows. The splatter of blood on the walls. She thought about all the people who had turned. All the people who had succumbed to the rage. Could Nisha have prevented that? And were there others out there like her?

And if it came to sacrificing Nisha for the sake of everyone...

No.

No, she couldn't think about that.

She couldn't even go there.

She'd sworn to protect Nisha.

She'd pledged to look after her.

She wasn't going to do anything that might jeopardise her safety in any way.

Theo cleared his throat. "Right. Not much further. So this is the end of the road for me." Although, in all honesty, Keira had lost track of where they were even heading. The North Lancs Barracks. That was it. This supposed safe place. The place where they had some kind of antidote.

What if the antidote was someone else like Nisha?

She walked up to Theo. Stood beside him. Looked around at him as he stood there, smelling like shit.

"I should thank you," Keira said.

Theo shrugged. "For what?"

"For helping us. Through the sewers. For getting us this far. I owe you a lot."

Theo looked at her with twitching eyes. "You can always stay with me. If you... have a change of heart."

Keira smiled. "And I appreciate that. Truly. But... you should maybe come with us. It sounds like it's a lot safer in this barracks than it is on the street."

Theo stared at her. Right into her eyes. She could see the whites of his eyes turning... bloodshot. He looked upset. Like he was about to start crying. She could hear Rufus growling, too, as thick clouds crept across the sky towards them.

"There's no place for me there," he said. And suddenly, he didn't sound like Theo. His entire demeanour... it'd changed. Drastically. And it gave Keira the creeps. It didn't make sense.

"What..." she started.

"I'm sorry. But it'll be worthwhile in the end," he said.

"I don't..."

And then, before Keira could even process what Theo was saying, he pulled out a dirty rag and wrapped it around Keira's mouth.

She tried to break free.

She tried to struggle free of his grip as Rufus barked and as Nisha ran towards her, wide-eyed.

But she felt a warmth surrounding her...

She felt that warmth seeping into her body, like a cup of tea on a cold day...

And then she felt...

Peace.

SETH

* * *

Seth held the nice lady Keira tight over his shoulder and he couldn't wait to get her back home,
Because she was the lady he'd been waiting to meet his entire life.

It was so nice and sunny. A perfect day. When he was younger, he wouldn't play out much when it was nice and sunny because that's the day when all the other children were out playing. He didn't like playing out when all the other children were playing out. Because they'd tease him, and they'd bully him, and they'd call him names. He didn't understand why they were like that with him. Why they were so mean to him.

But Mum always said he was *different* from the other children. So maybe that was the truth.

Maybe they didn't like him because he was just... different.

Mum never liked him going out in the summer. She told him he should stay inside where he was safe and couldn't be bullied or picked on. But Seth remembered one day, looking out of the front window and seeing Davey Walker with his shiny new bike. The bike looked so good. And Seth just wanted to ride it. And maybe if he rode it, Rachel Waterford might see him on it, and she might like him for it and not laugh at him for it, and if she *did* laugh at him for it, then he could think about how he just wanted her to be *quiet*.

And *how* he could quieten her.

His hands around her lovely neck.

Squeezing tight.

Bashing her head against the floor.

The thought made him hard.

He remembered peeking out of the window at that bike, trying not to get spotted, when suddenly Davey looked up at him. First, he nudged his friends, a couple of older boys who Seth didn't know. And Seth thought he might say something to him. Something nasty. Like he always did.

But then... Davey did something Seth didn't expect.

He spun his hand around. Rolled it around. Like he was telling him to open the window.

Seth wasn't sure what to do. Mum wouldn't be happy with him if he opened the window, would she?

But... Davey.

He didn't look like he was being mean. Even though he was *always* mean to Seth in school.

He looked like... he wanted to talk to him.

So Seth looked around. He heard Mum singing to herself downstairs. She was far away. He had plenty of time to open and close the window if he had to. He just had to hear what Davey had to say first.

He gulped.

He took a deep breath.

Then he grabbed the window, and he yanked it open.

The warm air rushed inside. And even though he was so used to being inside, even though he felt so safe inside... it was lovely. Lovely against his face. He could hear kids playing. He could hear dogs barking. And he could *feel* that warmth, getting warmer, warmer...

He looked down at Davey and his friends.

"Hey, Seth," Davey said. "Want a ride?"

Wow. Was this... Davey? Asking him if he wanted a ride on his brand-new bike? No. This couldn't be right. Things like this didn't happen to Seth. Only bad things happened to Seth.

"Come on," Davey said. "Sneak out. Your mum won't even know you've gone."

Wait. Sneak out? Was he...

Telling him to climb out the window?

He looked down. Down at the front garden.

It looked an awful long way down.

"Don't worry," one of the older lads said. "I jump out my window all the time. It looks far. But it's fine. Really."

Seth stood at the open window, and he took a deep breath of the warm summer air.

He looked at Davey and his two friends standing there and Davey's beautiful new bike.

He heard his mum humming away downstairs.

He could be in and out.

She'd never have to know.

"Come on!" Davey shouted. "Quick. We wanna get biking. You can come with us. An adventure, huh?"

And Seth smiled. Maybe Mum was wrong. Maybe he wasn't different. Maybe he was normal, and he'd just been unlucky. Maybe he'd been waiting for someone as nice and as kind as Davey all these years.

And maybe Davey really wasn't being mean to him. Maybe he wasn't "taking advantage of him," as Mum said.

Maybe he was just teasing him. Playing around with him. Mates did that sometimes, didn't they?

He stood at the edge of the window, and he took a deep breath of that warm summer air.

And then, he stepped over it...

He didn't know it was a bad idea until he realised he'd been falling for quite some time.

And then he hit the hard ground with a crunch, smashing one of Mum's pots in the process.

And while he was on the ground, while he was lying there, while the pain was so hard and he couldn't stop screaming, he saw Davey and his friends, all laughing at him, then Davey getting his thing out and weeing all over him as he lay there and—

"Seth!"

Davey suddenly spun around on his nice bike and cycled away. "The crazy bitch is here."

And as Seth lay there, hurting, so sore, crying so bad while his leg ached and his mouth tasted of blood, he just wanted Mum to hold him; he just wanted Mum to tell him he was okay, that everything was going to be okay.

But she looked down at him as he lay there stinking of wee, with anger in her eyes.

"How *dare* you leave the house," she said.

He held on to the nice lady Keira. He looked at the dog, barking at him, growling. And he looked at the girl, too. The little girl.

She would be a nice addition to his family.

The dog would be a nice addition to his family.

But they weren't the ones he wanted.

Keira was the only one he wanted.

The one he'd waited for his whole life.

He held Keira tighter, and he remembered her standing there on that warm summer day all those years ago.

Her and Rachel Waterford.

All those years ago.

He held on to her, and he heard Theo's voice deep inside.

Don't do this, Seth. It's not too late. Don't...

And then Seth took a deep breath, and Theo's voice disappeared.

There was no Theo anymore.

There was only Seth.

And it was time to take his new lady home.

NISHA

* * *

Nisha ran as fast as she could after Keira. Because the nasty man was taking her away from her.

And she couldn't let the nasty man take her away from her.

He was holding Keira. Carrying her. He'd put some blanket over her mouth, and she'd tried to shake away from it, tried to get away from him, but then her eyes closed, and her legs went like jelly, and she collapsed.

And now he was carrying her away.

She ran. Even though her feet hurt really bad, she ran. Even though she felt weaker than she'd ever felt before, she ran.

Because she couldn't let Keira go.

She couldn't let him take her.

But the man was running too. And he was running a lot faster than her. And he was getting further and further away. And Nisha couldn't let him get further and further away. She never liked the man. She always thought there was something weird about him. And it wasn't like her because she usually felt like everyone was good. Dad always said she was "too trusting" sometimes, but if you couldn't trust other people, then who could you trust?

But the man was getting further away. And the more she tried to run, the more the bloody taste filled her mouth. And the nasty taste from when she'd fallen into the sewer water, too. And also something else. Something salty. Tears.

She tightened her fists together.

She ran harder. But her legs were getting all stiff, and she didn't feel like she could run much further cause her belly was aching, everything was sore, and she couldn't breathe properly.

But she couldn't give up on Keira.

She had to keep running.

Keira. The bite. And then what Nisha had done. The darkness that the voice wanted her to go towards.

And... the light.

She'd gone towards the light. And she felt tired after it. Really tired.

She watched the man get further and further away. She looked to her side and saw Rufus. Running along with her. The hairs on his back all stood on end, like when Dad put the gel in his hair before he went bald and made it look all silly. Rufus was barking. And he was trying to run after the man too. And Keira. But even he didn't look like he could go any faster.

And she wanted to tell Rufus to run faster. To try harder. Because she felt too weak to run any faster. And if she couldn't run any faster... she couldn't help Keira.

She wanted Rufus to run off ahead. To bite the nasty man. To help Keira back. She pictured Keira riding on Rufus's back like he was a horse. A big, strong horse.

But instead, the man was just getting further and further away.

Keira was just getting further and further away.

And she and Rufus were getting no closer to catching up.

The man carrying Keira disappeared.

But Nisha didn't give up. She couldn't. She had to keep

running. She had to keep going. Even though her feet were so sore. Even though her legs were like heavy rocks. And even though her belly ached so bad, and even though she couldn't breathe any faster, and her heart felt like it was going to burst out of her chest... she couldn't give up.

She ran further and further until, eventually, she fell over onto the road.

She lay there. Face flat. She wanted to push herself up. So why couldn't she push herself up? She wasn't weak. She was strong. She was so strong. That's what Dad always told her.

So why couldn't she push herself up?

She lay there. On the road. Face flat on the concrete. And she felt more tears coming out of her eyes and tasted them on her lips. She lay there, her body shaking, her body broken, and she cried.

She lay there on the road, and she couldn't move another muscle.

She lay there, Rufus right beside her. Sitting there. Staring down the road. Panting. And she wanted to tell him to keep running. She wanted to scream at him to keep going. To get Keira back.

But she lay there, and she knew there was nothing else she could do.

There was nothing Rufus could do.

The man was gone.

Keira was gone.

KEIRA

* * *

Keira opened her eyes, and right away, she knew she was in deep shit.

She was... moving. Floating. Floating through the air. She tried to move her hands and twitch her toes, but they just wouldn't budge. She felt like she was out of battery. Like a phone, limping along at a couple of percent, trying to cling to life. But the more she tried to move, the more her exhaustion grew. The more she tried to move, the less capable of moving she felt.

She blinked a few times. Everything was... fuzzy. Cloudy. Furry, almost. It was hard to explain. But she sort of felt like she was in a cloud. A nice warm cloud. No. Not just *a* cloud. She was floating *with* the clouds in the sky. She could see a bright light somewhere up above. She could see a luscious blue.

And she could feel herself. Floating along. Not a care in the world.

Only that wasn't technically true, was it?

Because even though Keira was weak, even though she could

barely move a muscle, she knew something was desperately wrong.

A ringing noise blared through her ears. Like someone was standing beside her, ringing a bell louder and louder. She thought she could hear voices in the haze. She thought she could hear... singing.

Wait. Had she turned? She'd been bitten. Had the infected sunk its teeth into her? Was she wrong about Nisha *stopping* it, somehow? 'Cause that was crazy, wasn't it? Batshit crazy.

Fuck.

She took a deep breath. A faintly medicinal smell filled her nostrils. Something medicinal.

And something...

Sour.

She blinked again, a few more times.

And then, suddenly, with a click of a finger, she wasn't floating anymore.

She was in a living room. It was dusty. Dark. Some of the wallpaper was peeling away at the edges. A little damp crept up the wall in the far corner. There was a musty smell to the place. Like no fresh air had entered here in a long, long time. Old photographs lined the mantlepiece by the ancient fireplace. They were in black and white and looked like they'd faded.

Keira was sitting in some sort of old chair. She looked down. A couple of woodlice crept around her feet. She felt a shiver creep down her spine. She didn't like woodlice. Never had. They always struck her as distinctly alien beings. So, to see them creeping over her toes right now knocked her sick.

She shuffled her foot away. But she was still so tired. So exhausted. So weak. She took a few deep breaths. She had to steady herself. Calm herself. Something... something had happened on the road. Theo. He'd... attacked her. For no reason. And then he'd drugged her with something and dragged her away.

And now here she was. Sitting on this chair. Wearing... a white nighty. She didn't feel as grubby as earlier, either. Had Theo washed her? Cleaned her? Changed her?

What the hell was going on?

She tried to move her wrists. Expecting to find them clamped together.

But, much to her surprise... they just moved apart.

She wasn't bound up.

She was free to get out of this place.

Free to leave.

And as knackered and weak as she felt... that's exactly what she intended to do.

She swallowed a lump in her throat. Tried to stand. But her legs felt heavy. Her knees felt weak. Her feet just locked together, no matter how much she tried to move them. Fuck. She needed to get out of here. And she needed to get out of here fast.

What the fuck had that Theo fucker done to her?

Why?

And...

Where the hell were Nisha and Rufus?

She shuffled her feet around. Clenched on the sides of the chair arms. Dug her nails right in.

She took a deep breath.

Swallowed a lump in her throat.

And then she went to stand.

Footsteps.

Floorboards creaking somewhere above her.

She froze.

A numbness filled her body.

Her heart started racing.

Theo.

Theo was upstairs.

She wasn't alone.

She sat there. Frozen. The anxiety made her feel even weaker. Which wasn't good. It wasn't fucking good at all.

She needed all her strength right now.
She squeezed her burning eyes shut.
She swallowed a lump in her throat.
She took another long, deep breath.
Come on, Keira.
Now or never.

And then she tightened her grip on the chair and hauled herself to her feet.

She wobbled as she stood. Her knees were weak. Felt like jelly. And the second she stood, she went dizzy. She could feel herself tumbling. Feel herself falling. Feel herself...

No.
She was steady.
She was okay.
Everything was going to be okay.
She was going to find Nisha.
She was going to find Rufus.
And she was going to get out of here.
She took another deep breath.

Then she took a step across the dusty, worn-down living room carpet.

Towards the chipped old door.
She had to get to that door.
She had to get out of here.
Her feet were heavy.
Breathing was a struggle.
And every single step exhausted her.
But she kept on going.
She kept on...
More footsteps.
Creaking around above her.
She reached the door.
Grabbed the rusty handle.
Turned it.

Lowered it.

And then she pulled it open.

A dark hallway greeted her. She could see dust particles floating around in the air. Felt a sudden urge to sneeze.

But...

No.

She needed to be as quiet as possible.

She needed to get out of here.

She staggered around the side of the door.

She stumbled towards the frosted glass front door.

She needed to get out of here.

She needed to...

Suddenly, the next door on the left caught her eye.

It was ajar.

And even though every instinct in her body screamed at her to keep on running, to keep on going... something made her stop right there.

Something made her freeze.

Something made her peek through that crack in the door.

It looked like a dining room. It was dark in there. Curtains were pulled across the window, blocking the bulk of the light.

And it smelled musty, too. Damp.

And there was another smell in the air.

Two smells, actually.

That medicinal smell. So strong now.

And another smell.

The smell of...

Death.

She was about to step away from the door when suddenly, one of the silhouetted shapes in the room caught her eye.

A woman.

A woman in a nighty.

Sitting still at the table.

Holding a knife and fork.

A plate full of some sort of rotten food in front of her, which flies swarmed around and maggots clawed at.

She stood there, and her heart started racing.

A sickness punched her gut.

Because...

This figure.

And the other figures.

They were...

Dead.

She went to run away as fast as her weakened body would allow when suddenly, she heard footsteps right beside her.

She froze.

Her heart raced faster.

She didn't want to turn around.

She didn't want to look.

But at the same time... she knew she didn't have a choice.

She turned around slowly, and held her breath.

Theo stood opposite her, right at the foot of the stairs.

Blocking her way to the front door.

He smiled at her.

"Hello, Keira," he said. "Good to see you awake. Allow me to introduce myself. I'm Seth."

Wait. Seth? What... Why did she recognise that name?

How did she know him?

He walked over to the dining room door. Pushed it open. The stench filled Keira's lungs, making her heave.

Theo—or Seth, as he called himself—smiled. "And allow me to introduce you to my family. They've been looking forward to meeting you for so long. You're going to be spending a long, long time together..."

SARAH

* * *

Sarah looked over her shoulder and couldn't comprehend what she was looking at.

Which seemed a rather trite observation in a world where practically nothing seemed beyond comprehension anymore.

In the morning light, she could hear them. She could smell them. Inching closer and closer.

And even though she couldn't *see* them initially... she sure as shit could see them now.

The infected.

So many of them.

A crowd of them.

And they were all staggering down the road.

No.

Not staggering.

Racing down the road.

Racing towards her.

Her stomach turned. She hadn't seen a crowd like this since

that horrible moment when Keira lost David. When David died. Where Nisha lost consciousness.

And back then… somehow, Nisha had been able to divert them.

She'd been able to divert the horde.

Push it in another direction.

But now…

Nisha wasn't here anymore.

It was just her.

Just her and the crowd.

And she needed to get the hell away.

She turned around. She went to run. But the road stretched on long and far. She was going to grow tired. She was going to grow exhausted.

And the infected… they weren't going to get tired.

They weren't going to get exhausted.

They were going to keep on coming.

They were going to keep on chasing her.

She didn't stand a chance.

But what the fuck could she do? Stand here? Stand here and wait? Bide her time until the infected reached her?

Because she didn't have Nisha here with her anymore.

And she didn't have Carly here with her anymore.

She didn't have anything but herself.

She stood there. Shaking. Watching the crowd of infected racing closer. She saw them all, and she saw Harry stroking her thighs. She saw them all, and she saw Dean pushing her into the cupboard, punching her in the stomach, then making love—no, not love, it was anything but love—to her when she'd "served her punishment" for long enough.

She saw the incel bastards who tried to abuse her, who forced that monster dog upon her, and… Fuck. Her leg. That was going to slow her down even more.

She was fucked.

She was completely fucked.

Unless...

She looked around and saw the military vehicle right beside her.

It was a long shot. Driving any vehicle in this world was a risk. It drew too much attention. Way too much attention.

But right now, it might just be the lifeline she needed.

Fuck. What was there to lose?

She clambered onto the side of the military vehicle.

She scrambled around for the keys. Fuck. She couldn't see any keys. They must've taken them. Of course they must've...

And then she saw them.

A set of keys.

Right there by the accelerator.

Wow. What was this unfamiliar feeling?

This unfamiliar feeling of *luck*?

She reached down.

Grabbed the keys.

And then she stuck them into the car with her shaking hand.

Gripped the steering wheel and the handbrake tight.

"Come on," she said, starting up the engine. "Please, please give me some luck. Please."

She almost cringed at the futility of her hopes.

And then she turned the key, and...

The engine.

It spluttered to life.

She laughed. She actually laughed.

The vehicle.

It was alive.

It was alive, and she had a chance to get away from here.

For the first time since this whole outbreak began, something was *actually* going her way for once.

And then she saw something up ahead.

Something that made her realise her happiness was futile.

Figures.

Infected.

In the road.

Strays.

Running towards her.

Fuck.

She gritted her teeth.

She held onto the steering wheel.

She heard the infected crowd racing down the road towards her.

And she saw the infected approaching from up ahead.

"Fuck it," she said. "Now or never."

She didn't have a choice.

She didn't have a choice at all.

There was only one thing she could do.

And that was drive.

She slammed her foot on the gas and hurtled down the road.

She clutched the steering wheel tight.

The figures up ahead.

There were quite a few of them.

Running towards her.

And... shit, this was madness. This was total madness.

But if it was madness... why was she smiling?

Why was she smiling with tears creeping down her cheeks?

She felt the wind blowing against her face.

She felt her hair fluttering around her eyes.

She felt it all, and she smiled.

She was going to get out of this.

She was strong enough.

She saw the infected running towards the vehicle and tried to manoeuvre the car around them.

But the further she drove... the more she realised she wouldn't be able to.

She only had one choice.

She held her breath as the infected men and women inched closer.

She tightened her grip on the steering wheel and leaned back in the seat.

"Now or never," she said. "Now or…"

She slammed into the first infected.

Sent him splattering to the side of the road.

The vehicle rocked and shook from side to side. It slowed for a moment. Fuck. No. She couldn't slow down. She couldn't let that happen.

She needed to keep going.

She needed to keep driving.

She needed to keep—

Another infected slammed against the vehicle.

And then another.

And before she knew it, she was driving into a bunch of them.

Only…

Too many.

Far too many.

"Fuck."

She slammed her foot down harder on the accelerator and prayed for a break when suddenly, an infected man leaped onto the side of the vehicle.

He clung on as she drove.

Snarling.

Crying.

She kept her foot on the accelerator.

She lifted her other foot.

And then she booted him in the face.

Hard.

He kept on holding on.

"Fuck off," she said, swinging her foot at him again.

But he just wasn't budging.

"Fuck… off!" she shouted.

The man went hurtling off the side of the vehicle.

She saw his skin stripping from his face as it collided with the concrete.

And then she felt the car speeding up again, felt the resistance weakening. She was—she was moving again. She was moving. She was going to be okay. Everything was going to be okay.

She looked back at the infected, racing towards her.

She looked back at them all in the distance.

She took a deep breath, and she smiled.

She was strong.

She was going to be okay.

She was...

And then she felt the vehicle jolt to a halt.

She turned around. Stared at the steering wheel.

"No," she said. Grabbing the keys. Trying to start up the engine again.

The engine just coughed.

Spluttered.

Then died.

"No," Sarah said. "Not now. Not fucking now..."

She tried to start the vehicle again, but it failed.

She tried to spark it to life again, but it failed.

And as she sat there, she heard the infected groans and footsteps getting closer and closer and closer.

She was fucked.

She was completely and utterly fucked.

NISHA

* * *

Nisha wasn't sure how long she lay on the road holding Rufus.

It wasn't sunny anymore. At least it didn't *feel* sunny. It felt cold now. Rainy. Or maybe not. She wasn't sure. She was just sitting on the road, squeezing her eyes shut and stroking Rufus. She didn't want to see if the bad people were coming. She didn't care anymore.

She just wanted to wait here.

She just wanted to wait here in the dark.

And if the bad people got her, well, the bad people got her, and that had to be okay.

Because if the bad people got her, at least she could see Dad again.

At least she would be able to see...

Keira again.

She thought about the man. The man who took her away. The nasty man. The way he threw her over his shoulder and then ran away.

And Nisha *tried* to chase him.

She tried so hard to chase him.

But it didn't matter how hard she tried.

Her legs just gave way underneath her.

Her body just went weak underneath her.

And she fell to the road, and now she was on the road, and she was crying, and she just couldn't stop crying.

She lay there, and she saw these words flashing in her head. And they were being signed to her. They were being signed to her by George Wilson, Fatima Patel, and many other people from school.

And they were all saying she was useless.

They were all laughing at her, and they were all telling her she was so, so useless.

Because, yes, she'd been able to keep the bad people away for a bit.

But now she couldn't.

Now, she couldn't, and she didn't know what she was supposed to do without those powers if they were what they were.

'Cause she was just... normal without them.

No.

Not normal.

She was worse than normal.

She was deaf, and she was stupid, and she was useless, and she was...

Don't worry dear you're not useless we've got you we're here we're here we're always here...

And she *heard* that voice, then.

That voice.

The one she hadn't heard for so long.

You've been silly you've done silly things but now you can help us now you can help yourself now we can help you...

And hearing that voice, it reminded her of what she'd done.

The way she'd held Keira's hand. The way she'd seen that darkness. The way she'd reached for the light.

And the way she'd felt the badness disappearing from Keira.

She'd *done* that.

But there was also something else.

Something she didn't want to think about.

The darkness.

Yes the darkness yes that's where you go you're strong enough now you're...

She felt that darkness, and she thought of the man. The man who'd taken Keira away. The man who'd carried her over her shoulder.

And she wanted to get him.

She wanted to get him, and she wanted to show him how strong she was.

She wanted to look in his eyes while he sat on the ground and tell him she was *Nisha* and she was strong and—

Yes so strong so so strong so...

She opened her eyes.

She looked down the road. Where the man had run with Keira over his shoulder.

She looked to her side and saw Rufus... looking at her.

But he wasn't looking at her in that friendly way anymore.

He was looking at her like he didn't like her again.

And it was right when she *felt* the words that he looked at her that way.

Like he *knew*.

She stood there. Her hands were shaking. And she felt so tired. So, so tired.

But she also felt... strong again.

She stood there in the clouds.

Stood there in the rain.

And she looked down the road, right down the road, towards where the man had taken Keira.

And she could see where she had to go.

She could see his footprints.

His muddy footprints on the road.

And as she stood there, tired, exhausted, and wanting to sleep more than anything... she didn't feel weak anymore.

She didn't see the kids who laughed at her and teased her standing opposite her. Signing at her. Laughing at her.

She saw them with their throats cut.

She saw them bleeding out everywhere.

She saw them begging for their lives.

Yes dear yes don't resist accept don't resist...

She swallowed a lump in her throat.

She took a deep breath.

She looked down at Rufus, who turned away from her and showed his teeth.

And even though she felt different... she realised she wasn't less than normal.

She wasn't weak.

She was strong.

I'm coming for you, Keira.

I'm coming for you.

And then she walked.

KEIRA

***

Keira listened to the words Theo—or was it Seth?—said, but she couldn't really take any of them in.
Because she was afraid.
She stood by the entrance to this dining room. This hellish fucking dining room in this awful, damp, dark house. She could see someone in the dining room. More than one person, come to think about it, sat around the table.

And every one of them?
Dead.
Sat at the table.
Stiff.
A woman.
A man.
A child.
And... more of them, too.

Suddenly, the rotting stench grew even worse. That medicinal punch clearly poured to try and reduce the intensity. But actually making it even more acrid. Even worse.

It was strong. It was so fucking strong.

It made Keira want to vomit.

It made Keira want to heave.

But all she could do was stand there.

All she could do was stare at this *Seth*, as he now called himself, since his demeanour had shifted so drastically.

"I should apologise for not introducing myself earlier," he said. "Theo sometimes likes to... take the lead. In social situations."

Fuck. He was a lunatic. This guy was fucked in the head. He'd seemed so... well, not entirely *normal* as Theo. But he seemed to have his shit together.

And now...

Now, he seemed insane.

No. He *was* insane.

He had dead fucking bodies sitting around a table.

Of course, he was insane.

"What have you done with Nisha?" Keira asked. She needed to stay measured. She needed to stay calm. She knew dealing with pricks like this wasn't ordinary. You had to play their own game a little. You had to get them right where you wanted them.

And that's what she had to do.

Even though she was fucking terrified.

Seth, as she now saw him, sighed. "The girl is fine. I think."

"What do you mean by that?"

"The girl can... look after herself," Seth said. "And if she can't, the dog can protect her."

What did he mean by that? Was Nisha still out there on the road? Was she on her own? Or was he lying? It was impossible to tell how serious he was being. Impossible to decipher him.

"But we don't need to worry about them right now," he said, smile widening. "You're here. And that's the main thing, isn't it, Keira? After all these years... you're finally here."

Finally here? What was this prick on about?

"I don't... I don't understand."

"You don't remember me?" he asked. And there was a pain in his eyes, then. A sadness. And that sadness worried her. She didn't want to upset him. She wanted to keep him on side. For as long as she could.

There was something about him that she remembered. But she just couldn't figure it out. She couldn't quite place him. But he *was* familiar.

"You don't remember that time you helped me up? When Mum... When Mum was mean to me?"

And then, suddenly, in a flash, it all came back to her.

Summer. Summer as a kid. Walking down the street with her friends at the time. Rachel. Annie. Seeing this boy lying on the ground, crying. Holding his ankle. It was a warm day, but he was shivering. He didn't look well. He didn't look well at all.

That's creepy Seth, Rachel said.

And as much as the kid did look a bit unusual... Keira felt sorry for him.

So she went over to him. She asked him if he was okay. She told him her name. She asked if he needed an ambulance, and he insisted he didn't. If she called an ambulance, he'd be in trouble with Mum. Big trouble.

So she didn't call that ambulance. But she held his hand. She stroked the back of his hand.

He looked up at her like she was the first person who'd ever showed any care towards him in his life.

And now here he was.

Right in front of her.

"When I saw you," Seth said, "I didn't believe it was you. I mean... what are the chances? All these years. All this time. And now here you are. Keira. After all these years."

A sickly taste filled Keira's lips. The way he looked at her. The delight with which he saw her. She'd almost feel sorry for him. If he didn't have a bunch of dead bodies in the dining room. And hadn't fucking kidnapped her.

"Yes," Keira said. "I remember."

Seth shook his head. Started muttering under his breath. "No, no, no. She doesn't remember. She doesn't remember. Stupid. Like the others. Stupid, like..."

"Summer," Keira said. "Seeing you on the ground. Holding your hand. I remember. I just... I have a bad memory at first. That's all."

His eyes glistened. He looked at her like he didn't trust her. Like he'd been betrayed a ton of times in his life, and he wasn't sure whether to believe her or not.

"I remember," Keira said. Smiling. Or at least forcing a smile. Maybe if she were nice to him, she could make him see. Maybe if she were nice to him... he'd let her go. He'd see sense. Eventually.

He walked towards her. Slowly.

Walked right up to her.

He smelled of the sewer water, still. And it made her feel sick.

He reached up. Touched her face with his cold, damp fingers.

"All these years," he said. "And you remember me."

She smiled back at him. Fuck. Nisha. What did she say? What could she possibly say to this guy? The Theo side of him... he seemed rational. He seemed logical.

But the *Seth* side...

"I always knew we'd meet again," he said. "I always knew you'd visit my home someday. I always knew we'd be happy together. You and me. Because—because you're the only one who understands me. Don't you see? You're the only one who *sees* me. You're the only one who ever saw me."

Okay. The more he spoke, the more worried Keira grew. 'Cause it sounded like this guy was obsessed with her. It was years ago. Twenty years ago. And he was speaking about that moment like it was *fate*.

Again, sad. But also... creepy.

She stood there. His cold fingers against her face. Her heart racing. The taste of vomit growing in her mouth. Getting stronger and stronger, more and more acidic.

"I always knew we'd meet again. I always knew I'd get the chance to bring you home. To introduce you to Mum. To... the others."

The way he said *the others*. It partly sounded like he loved them.

But it also sounded like he detested them.

It was a fine balance.

"You look so beautiful," he said, stroking his fingers against her face even more. I think it's time for you to meet them. Don't you?"

He put a hand on her back.

She felt a shiver down her spine.

She felt the vomit touch the back of her throat.

And he pushed her towards the door.

"Come on," he said. "Don't be afraid. It's time for you to meet my people. It's time for you to meet my family."

She stepped inside the dining room.

And suddenly, when she saw the people sitting around the table clearly, she understood.

She knew she was in deep shit before.

But now...

Seeing this table.

Seeing these people...

She was in far deeper shit than she first realised.

SARAH

* * *

Sarah sat in the broken-down military vehicle, listening to the infected racing towards her.

Was her luck finally out?

She could hear the infected shrieking, groaning, screaming as they ran down the road towards her. She could hear her heartbeat racing in her skull, the blood whooshing through her ears. Up ahead, the road stretched on. Endless. Trees either side of her. But nowhere to hide.

She was a sitting duck.

She stared down the road, her hands shaking, her entire body numb. Nerves clawed at her gut like ants, creeping their way around her insides. The infected's groans and cries grew closer.

And all she could do was sit there.

Frozen.

Frozen, like she was lying on the ground opposite that wall as a child.

Frozen, like she was locked away in that cupboard, waiting for Dean's return.

She clutched the steering wheel. She couldn't move her fingers. They were frozen. Glued to the wheel. Fuck. Why couldn't she move them? She needed to peel her hands away from the wheel. And she needed to get out of this car. She needed to run.

But... her hands wouldn't move.

Her legs wouldn't move.

Nothing would move.

She was frozen to the spot.

Her heart pounded in her chest. She felt it in her neck, too, and all over her body. The dirty scent of the infected inched closer, making her insides turn. It was typical, really, wasn't it? It was inevitable. She always froze when it mattered most. Always.

She could *try* to convince herself she was strong.

She could *try* to lie to herself that she wasn't weak.

But in the end, the truth always reared its ugly head.

She was a freezer.

And there was nothing she could do to change that.

She sat there, gripping hold of the steering wheel, when suddenly, an image of Nisha flashed in her mind.

Carly.

Carly's words.

Carly's *final* words.

The things she'd told her about Nisha.

Why it was so, so dangerous if this Leonard character got his hands on her.

But more than that.

She cared about Nisha.

And she cared about Keira, too.

And, most unexpectedly... she cared about Rufus.

A warm tear crept down her cheek.

Rufus.

Keira.

Nisha.

She couldn't give up on them.

She had to find them.

She couldn't just give up on them.

She sat there. Hands frozen to the wheel. Feet frozen to the bottom of the vehicle. Heart pounding. Not breathing.

Just breathe.

Just breathe...

The infected cries echoed closer.

Their footsteps hammered against the road.

So many of them.

An entire crowd of them.

But she couldn't give up.

Just breathe, Sarah.

Just breathe.

She sat there. Shaking violently.

The infected ran closer.

And closer.

Just breathe.

Just...

And then, suddenly... a gasp of air filled her lungs.

Her hands loosened from the steering wheel.

Her feet finally—fucking finally—moved.

And she launched herself out of the military vehicle and onto the road.

She started running. Her ankle ached so bad. Fuck. She kept forgetting about the dog bite.

But... fuck, she couldn't think about the dog bite right now. She had to try and keep on moving through the pain.

Because if she didn't, she was dead.

Fuck. She was dead anyway.

But she had to keep going.

She had to keep running.

The infected screamed even louder when she climbed out of the vehicle. It was as if they'd grown excited. They'd seen her, and they had grown excited. They were hunting her. Hunting their prey.

Fuck. Just breathe. Just keep breathing.

She ran down the road. Her feet hit the concrete. Every step felt like wading through tar. The pain in her leg growing stronger. And the crippling pain in her back, too, growing, intensifying...

No.

Not now.

Keep running.

Keep going.

Keep—

She stumbled forward.

Lost her balance.

Fell face flat on the road.

Fuck. She needed to get up. And she needed to get up fast.

Because if she didn't get up...

The infected's cries got louder.

Their footsteps grew closer.

She didn't want to turn around. She couldn't turn around.

She had to keep on running.

She had to get up.

A flash in her mind.

The ground beside the wall.

Her frozen, broken body...

No.

Not again.

Not *fucking* again.

She pushed herself to her feet and staggered down the road.

She couldn't run anymore. She could only limp. And the infected. They were so close behind. She wasn't turning around. If they caught up with her, they caught up with her. If this was the end, then this was the end.

But she wasn't giving up.

She wasn't a quitter.

If this was the end of her—which, let's face it, looked a realistic conclusion to jump to—then she wasn't going down screaming.

She was going down *running*.

Running as fast as she fucking could.

Which might not be very fast because of the state of her ankle and the pain in her body.

But she wasn't giving up.

She staggered down the road. Almost stumbled over again. The infected were so close now. Their stench seeping up her nostrils. Their taste filling her mouth.

Keep going.

Keep running.

Keep…

A sudden bolt of pain split down her spine.

She tumbled forward.

Slammed against the road.

Hard.

Her nose cracked against the concrete.

She tasted blood.

She had to get up.

She had to get the fuck back up to her feet.

She had to…

And then she felt a hand.

Against her back.

And the screams of the infected surrounded her.

KEIRA

* * *

Keira stepped into the dining room and immediately realised she was in far greater trouble than she first thought.

The dining room was much like the living room of this grotty old house. It was dark. The curtains were drawn, holding back the light. It looked like they hadn't been opened for years. There were cobwebs everywhere, many of them dancing with flies. The sound of buzzing flies filled the room. Or was that just the ringing in her ears? It was hard to tell.

A silhouette sat at the old wooden dining table. No, a series of silhouettes. All sitting there in the darkness. Sitting very still.

They all had plates in front of them. Knives and forks in their hands.

And their meals were covered in flies.

A sour stench filled the air. Made Keira feel dizzy. A few flies banged into her face, which she wafted away.

And all the while, she could hear this breathing right behind her.

Seth.

A cold hand against her back.

Stroking her.

Blocking her way out.

"It's such an honour for you to meet my mother. And for you to meet my special friends."

Seth's mum and his "special friends" were all sitting around the table. They were completely still. Not moving a muscle.

They were dead.

And their eyes were missing.

Their faces were covered in blood.

Tears of blood.

Keira's heart raced faster. The man. The man in the cellar. The one who told her about the "man in the attic".

It made sense.

It all suddenly made sense.

Seth.

Seth was the man in the attic.

And that man was one of his victims.

She looked around.

A woman and a child sat there at the table. Both next to each other. A woman, her head completely shaven. And a little boy or girl, it was hard to tell 'cause her head was shaven too.

But the way Seth had positioned them... the woman's arm around the kid...

It made shivers creep down Keira's spine.

Seth nudged her back so gently with his ice-cold fingers. "Come on. We've got a seat at the table for you."

Keira's skin went cold. She didn't want to take another step into this dining room. She wanted to turn around. She wanted to get the hell out of here.

But...

She had to play this right.

She had to lull Seth into a false sense of security.

And then she had to get the fuck out of here.

She took a deep breath. The stench of death clawed into her lungs, making her heave.

"Come on," Seth said. "You take a seat. Then we can start our meal."

She swallowed a thick lump of saliva.

She could do this.

She could navigate this.

One way or another, she was getting through this.

She walked towards the table. There was an empty place. And it had... *her* name on it. The hairs on her arms stood right on end. What the fuck? How long had this guy been waiting for her?

Seth pulled her chair out. Held out a hand, signalling her to sit. "Please. And if you're not comfortable, I can get you a cushion. Anything to help."

She swallowed back vomit. She nodded. "Thank you."

Seth nodded back at her. He smiled. "I'll... I'll get you some food. You stay right here, okay? You don't go anywhere."

And then he scooted off out of the dining room.

Keira stood there. Heart racing. This was her chance. Her chance to get to the front door. Her chance to run.

This table.

Surrounded by the dead.

Flies headbutting her.

And the *stench*...

She had to get out of here.

She had to get away.

Now.

She went to turn around when she saw him standing at the door.

Seth.

Holding a plate.

A plate of cold-looking meat and rancid vegetables.

Flies crawling all over it.

"Don't worry about the flies," he said, wafting them away. "They'll go away. And they aren't dirty. I've eaten them before, and they've never made me sick."

He walked over to the table.

Put the plate of rotting food out in front of her.

The smell made her eyes water and knocked her for six.

But she had to stay calm.

She had to keep her composure.

Seth stroked her back again. He smiled at her. "Take a seat. Please."

She looked at him.

His smiling face.

Then she looked around the room for something she could use to attack him with.

For *anything* she could use to attack him.

She saw the knives and forks on the table. But they looked way too blunt. Way too flimsy.

And that was it.

There was nothing else.

The moment had passed.

"Sit," he said. Pressing a little harder against her back now. "Please." But it didn't sound like an encouragement. It sounded like a threat this time.

She nodded. Just play the game, Keira. Just play the game...

She sat down on the creaky old wooden chair. At the head of the table. Three bodies to her left and three to her right. Like dolls. Mannequins.

Seth crept around the side of the table. He pulled out a chair. Right opposite her. Then he grabbed a lighter and lit a candle in the middle of the table. The smell of the sweet cherry cut through the sickliness, somehow making it even worse.

He put the lighter down on the table right beside him.

That was something she could use.

If she got the chance.

He stared across the table at her.

Smile widening.

Revealing missing teeth, yellow teeth, blackened teeth.

He grabbed his knife and fork as the candle flickered against his face.

The empty eye sockets of these people Keira was trying her hardest not to look at, staring right ahead of them.

"I've waited so long for this moment, my love," he said.

And then he sliced a piece of the rotting meat right in front of him as flies crawled along the fork.

"Now eat."

NISHA

* * *

Nisha wasn't sure how long she'd been walking when she lost track of the footprints.

It was sunny again. It was afternoon. Or at least it felt like afternoon anyway. Nisha could see a lot of cars that looked all smashed up. She couldn't see anyone in them. The windows of the houses on the road had pieces of wood covering them, too. And birds were flying over, nasty crows that looked like they wanted to swoop down and take her eyes out.

She remembered seeing a baby lamb with its eyes plucked out by a crow once. It made her feel sad. She wanted to help it. But there was nothing she could do for it.

When she went past it the next day, it wasn't there.

When she got to the farm, she saw it lying dead on the ground, with a line of other lambs.

She could smell a few things. The nasty water from the sewer still on her body and Rufus's fur, too. And she could smell burning somewhere. Which was worrying. Because if something was burning, it meant people were nearby. And she wasn't sure she wanted to bump into any people just yet.

Her mouth felt all dry. Her teeth felt all weird. She could taste blood, too. She didn't like the taste of blood. It made her feel sick. It reminded her of when she went into the bad people's bodies and what they liked doing to other people.

Biting other people.

Chewing other people.

Her heart started beating fast.

She hoped she wouldn't have to go into a bad person's body again.

Her feet were sore. She felt all shaky like jelly. And her tummy felt sickly. She felt a bit like she wanted to be sick. And her bite was hurting, too. It was burning. She hoped it wasn't infected. She was scared of infection. Ever since Dad's shoulder got infected 'cause he picked a spot, and it went all red and made him so poorly, she was so scared of infection.

She stood in the middle of the road. Rufus stood beside her. He didn't seem as scared of her now. He looked at her. Wagged his tail. So he liked her again.

She knew why he didn't like her sometimes. It was when she *felt* the voice inside her.

It was like Rufus could *tell*.

Like he just *knew* there was something different about her.

She didn't want to hear the voice again. It scared her.

But there was something else about the voice.

Even though it scared her... something about it made her feel...

Strong.

She stood there. Rufus looked up at her.

She looked around at the road.

Cars.

Boarded-up houses.

But no sign of the footprints anymore.

No sign of the nasty man who'd taken Keira.

She felt her lips wobbling. She felt her eyes going all blurry. She was too weak. She wasn't strong enough. She wasn't...

No.

She *was* strong enough.

She took a deep breath, and even though she didn't know where she was going, even though she didn't know how she was going to find Keira or what she was going to do when she did find her... she had to stay strong.

She was going to keep going.

She was going to keep trying.

She was going to...

And then she saw something.

Up ahead.

Right up the road.

She saw... something.

Blood.

Blood that looked like it'd trickled from someone onto the ground.

And then...

Muddy, damp footprints.

And the *smell* of the sewer water strong in the air.

She looked at the house.

She swallowed a big lump in her throat.

It was... it was Keira.

She stood there.

Tucked her fingernails into her palms.

She took a deep breath.

And then she walked towards the house.

It was time to be strong.

It was time to help her friend.

SARAH

* * *

Sarah hit the road, and the infected screams surrounded her.

The bodies of the infected huddled around her. She saw their pale faces, smeared with blood. She saw their bite marks, some of them on the neck, some of them across the face, some of them on the shoulder. Men. Women. Children. Old and young. All races. So many of them. Hovering right above her.

Their screams were deafening. But they weren't just screaming. They were growling. Shouting inaudible mutterings.

And some of them were saying things, too.

Like they were begging.

Like they were suffering.

Like they were mimicking the living in their final moments.

The smell was almost unimaginably bad. A combination of bitter vomit and putrid rot. It reminded her of when she'd found a dying sheep as a kid. Heard this pitiful cry. Looked down the slope and saw it lying there, legs broken. A chunk of flesh had been torn from its side. Blood oozed from that wound, trickling down its dirty white fluff.

She wanted to climb down that slope. She wanted to help the sheep. She wanted to comfort it in its misery, at least.

But all she could do was stand there and look down the slope. The knowledge gnawing at her that no matter how much she wanted to get down to that sheep, to help it... she couldn't. Because her back was crippled. Her whole body was crippled. There was nothing she could do.

She lay there on her back. A bitter taste filled her mouth, a combination of the stench and the taste of adrenaline.

And the infected.

Descending towards her.

In slow motion.

She held her breath. Her heart raced. Time stood still.

And all she could do was lie there.

All she could do was hold her breath.

All she could do was wait...

She was on the road, just like she was when she was a child, Harry perched over her.

She was on the floor, just like she was in the supermarket, when the infected surrounded her.

She was on the road.

But this time, she wasn't getting away.

This time, she wasn't getting out.

This time, she was...

She clenched her eyes shut.

She tensed her fists.

She waited for the agony.

She had no idea how long she'd been lying there. Fists clenched. Holding her breath. Heart racing.

But...

She couldn't feel any agony splitting through her body.

And come to think of it... she couldn't even *hear* the infected.

Snarling.

Growling.

Screaming.

She lay there. Heart pounding. Eyes squeezed shut. Darkness engulfing her.

She didn't want to open her eyes.

She didn't want to look.

But something wasn't quite *normal* here.

She swallowed a bitter lump in her throat.

Then she opened her eyes.

The sun shone down brightly from above. She could see a few birds fluttering by. Hear them singing, too. And it was beautiful. It was really quite beautiful.

Everything was so peaceful.

Everything was so... quiet.

She looked around, and she saw something else.

The infected.

They were all...

Frozen.

Frozen still.

Not moving a muscle.

They stood over her. They looked down at her. Or were they looking *through* her? It was almost... as if they couldn't see her. As if they'd lost her. As if she were invisible now.

Her heart started racing again. Because this... this was like the supermarket. When she fell down towards the floor and lay there on her back.

The infected were frozen again.

They weren't moving again.

They were... frozen.

She lay there. Shaking. She didn't want to move a muscle. 'Cause she felt like if she moved a muscle, they might see her, and they might attack her. She didn't want to take any chances right now. Any at all.

The infected stayed there. Frozen above her. Unspeaking. Unmoving. Completely static.

And the longer she lay there, the more her sense of urgency began to intensify.

She had to get up.

She had to get away.

She had to go.

She gulped.

Then she pushed herself to her feet.

The infected stayed frozen. Like statues. They weren't moving. They weren't moving a muscle.

She stood up further. A shooting pain hurtled up her spine. No. No, she couldn't succumb to the pain right now. She had to get up. She had to get going. She had to get the hell away from here. Now.

She turned around. Slowly. Clutching her back.

She saw the stray infected lingering in front of her. Also frozen.

She stood there, and she looked around, and she wondered what the hell was happening. What the actual hell was happening?

They were frozen.

Which usually meant one thing.

Just one thing.

Someone like Nisha was close.

Someone like Nisha was...

She turned around, and then, right ahead, in the distance, she saw it.

She saw it right in front of her, and her mouth went dry.

She saw it right in front of her, and her heart began to race.

She saw it right in front of her... and even though it didn't make sense, she understood.

Even though she didn't want to believe it... it made sense.

She understood.
Carly was right.
Carly was telling the truth.
Everything she'd told her was right.
And that changed everything.

KEIRA

* * *

Keira sat at the table with the plate of rotting meat in front of her and wondered just how far she would have to go to keep Seth on side.

The dining room was dark and dingy. Daylight shone in through the dusty, hole-filled cream curtains. Spiders crawled along in the corners of the wall and the ceiling. Having a feast on the flies that were unfortunate enough to fly up towards their webs.

She saw Seth sitting opposite her. Slicing away at that tough, burned meat. She saw flies dancing on his fork. He didn't seem to notice. He didn't seem to care.

And she saw the dead bodies perched either side of them at this dining table.

They were sitting upright. Solid. Rigor mortis had clearly set in. They stunk. A sourness to the air that never got old. That never wore off. It was usually the case when you smelled something bad that you grew used to it after a while.

But not this smell.

This smell was ghastly.

And it was getting worse and worse.

She felt dizzy. Her head ached like mad. She could hear the buzzing filling the air. And she could see Seth sitting across the table with his knife and fork in his hand.

And that smirk on his face.

Those wide eyes. Peering out at her.

"Go on," he said. "Tuck in. We don't want it going to waste, do we?"

She sat there. Head spinning. The stench and the adrenaline and *everything* just swirling around and combining and making her want to get up, making her want to run, making her want to—

She stood up.

Her heart racing.

Dizziness taking over.

Seth's face turned. "Keira?"

Keira's head spun. Especially hearing him say her name. It made her dizzy. It made her weak.

He stood up. Walked over towards her. "Are you..."

"I just need air," she said. Stepping away. Holding up her hands.

Seth walked towards her slowly. "What—"

"I need air. Okay?"

He stood there. Right opposite her. His eyes were wide. He held up his hands. He almost looked... scared. Startled by her sudden shift. By her panic.

He stood there. Not moving. Kept on holding up his hands. "Is there... is there anything I can get you?"

She looked around at the table.

At that lighter. The one he'd lit the candles with. One of which had flickered out already.

It was something.

But it wasn't enough.

She needed something else.

She needed...

She saw it sitting in the corner of the room.

The furniture polish.

Quite an irony. Considering this place looked like it hadn't seen any polish in an eternity. Or any kind of cleaning, for that matter.

But it was an aerosol can. And combined with the lighter... it could be something she could use.

As a weapon.

A hand.

A bony hand against her arm.

She looked around.

Seth.

"You don't have to worry, dear. You're safe from the monsters in here. You're safe from everything in here. From everyone in here. This is our safe place. This is where we've always meant to be. This is where *you're* always meant to be."

She stood there, and she felt his hand against her arm, squeezing, tightening. And she wanted to throw up. She wanted to tell him to get off her. To get the fuck off her. She wanted to tell him he was a creep. She wanted to tell him he was a psycho.

But then she saw the dead bodies, and she saw a reminder of what could happen to her if she wasn't careful.

What could happen to her if she didn't play things right.

She stood there, and she felt him wrapping his arms around her.

"Come on. Come here. For a hug. A hug will help you feel better. A hug will help everything go away..."

She wanted to push him away.

She wanted to get his hands away from her.

She wanted to push him to the floor and get the fuck out of this house...

But she let him hug her.

She let him wrap his arms around her.

He squeezed her. Tight. And she could hear him groan a little bit as he grabbed hold of her. As he moved his hands down her back. And she could feel something, too.

Something hard.

Digging into her leg.

And getting harder...

Fuck.

This creep was obsessed with her.

"It's okay," he said as he held her tighter. "I've got you now. I'm right here. You're right where you're always supposed to be."

She saw that lighter.

Just out of reach.

She reached out for it as she hugged him back with her right arm.

She reached closer towards it as she kissed the side of his neck, and then she felt her fingers touch it as she reached the table.

She grabbed it.

Grabbed it as he kissed her cheek.

And she moved it closer towards her, and...

Suddenly, she felt a crack.

A splitting crack.

Right across her left arm.

And then, before she even had the chance to realise what was happening, Seth was holding her and pushing her against the chair.

And then grabbing her face.

Grabbing her face and squeezing it tight as she sat there in that chair, staring up at him, peering into her eyes.

He looked down at her.

Tears in his eyes.

And he was...

He was holding on to the lighter now.

He was holding on to the lighter, and he was looking down at her. His jaw shaking.

"What—" she muttered. Trying to protest her innocence.

"You've tried to hurt me," he said.

Keira tried to shake her head. "No. No, I wasn't—"

He slapped her. Hard.

"You tried to grab the lighter. And you wanted to hurt me with it."

Keira shook her head again. "Seth. I didn't. Please. Let's..."

And then she saw something that made her shiver.

Seth.

Lifting something out of his pocket.

A long, bloody knife.

"I just wanted you to love me," he said. "I just wanted *someone* to love me. And it had to be you. It had to be you."

"I... I do love you, Seth. I do—"

"No!" he shouted with an almost childlike scream. "You're just like the others. You're just like everyone else. You don't love me. No one can ever love me. Everyone just... everyone just wants to hurt me."

He held that knife out in front of her. And she could feel his mood shifting. She could feel a change of tactic with him was necessary. But she wasn't even sure she was going to have the chance. She wasn't sure if the moment had already passed.

"No one can ever love me," he said, shifting that knife towards her. "But... but maybe I can love you. If you're silent. Like the rest of them. And if you don't look at me with those eyes. Like the rest of them."

It took Keira a moment to clock what he was getting at.

But as he moved that knife towards her, slowly, she caught a glimpse of the dead around the table and thought of the man in the cellar, and it all made sense.

"Everything will be quiet soon," he said. "Everything will be happy soon. Everything will be silent soon."

And then he moved the knife towards her throat.

KEIRA

* * *

Seth pressed the knife against Keira's throat and stared deeply into her eyes.

And as menacing as he looked, it was pity Keira felt for him.

Pure pity.

The knife dug hard into her neck. She tried to gulp, but she couldn't because it was pushing down too hard. It felt like, in no time at all, it might slice through her skin. Open her up. In no time at all, she was going to be bleeding out all over the place.

Tears crept down Seth's face. His mouth twitched. His breath stunk of shit. His teeth were yellow, covered in tartar. When she'd first seen him—and seen him as Theo—she hadn't noticed just how gross he was. Or maybe the way he'd carried himself came across more like a bloke who just didn't care much about what people thought about him.

But now... seeing him as *Seth*... she was repulsed by him.

"All these years," he said. "All these years, and I've *tried* to be better. I've *tried* to be different. I've *tried* to be like Theo. But I... I just can't. Because I always win. Seth always wins. And that's why I need you to be quiet, Keira. That's why I need you to be quiet."

She opened her mouth. But no sound came out. Just a pathetic gasp. She'd fucked up. She'd had one opportunity to get the fuck out of this house, and she'd fucked it. Royally.

She could hear the flies buzzing around the living room, driving her crazy. The smell of Seth's breath combined with the rotting, awful stench of the dead bodies. And in her mind's eye, she could only think of Nisha. Nisha and Rufus. Wherever the hell they were.

She prayed this bastard hadn't hurt them. She prayed he'd only kidnapped her.

And she prayed the pair of them stayed far, far away.

She felt the knife press harder against her neck. She could feel her pulse vibrating in her throat. She wanted to fight. She wanted to fight this awful, pitiful fucker.

But all she could do was sit there as he squeezed her cheeks.

All she could do was sit there as he pushed that knife against her with his shaking hand.

All she could do was sit there as the flies buzzed around her.

"We will be happy, you and me," he said. "If it's the last thing I do... it'll be to make sure you and me are happy. I'll look after you. I'll protect you. I'll be here for you, dear. Always."

She looked into his bloodshot eyes. She tried to move. She tried to shake free.

He pushed the knife down harder.

So hard she felt like her neck was going to burst.

"Don't look at me like that," he said.

Keira shook her head. Tried to speak. She couldn't breathe. She was going dizzy. Colours were filling her eyes. She felt sick. She felt shaky. She felt like she was going to pass out. She couldn't pass out. Passing out was what he wanted. Passing out was exactly what he...

And then suddenly, he yanked the blade away from her neck.

He grabbed her hair.

Leaned in close.

Leaned right into her ear as she gasped for air and felt his hot breath all over the side of her face, all over her neck.

"Don't look at me like that," he said again.

And she didn't realise what he was talking about. She didn't know how she was supposedly looking at him. She didn't know she was looking at him any way at all.

And then he slammed her head back.

Pushed the blade to her cheek this time.

And he looked into her eyes with this ferocious intensity.

"Don't look at me like that," he said. "Close your eyes. Close your dirty eyes, or I'll take them away. Like I took Theo's eyes away. I'll take them away!"

And she didn't even think. She swung at him. Clawed his face. And she felt her fingernails scratch across his face, and one of them poked his eyeball.

He yelped, and she tried to seize the moment as an opportunity to get away. A chance to run.

But it was no use.

He slapped her arm back.

He pushed her off the chair.

Sat on her chest as she lay back on the dusty floor, which woodlice scurried across.

And he pushed the knife against her right eye.

And then he moved a hand over her mouth.

"Be silent," he said. "Everything will be so much better when you're silent. Everything will be so much happier when you're silent. Everything will be okay..."

She tried to shake her head because she could see where that knife was moving towards.

She tried to break free of his grip because she could see it descending down.

Down towards her eyeball.

She tried to break free of him, and she tried to get away as the blade inched closer towards her eyeball.

"That's it," he said. A smile creeping across his face. Drool rolling down his chin. And a tear creeping from his right eye. "My silent girl. My beautiful, silent girl."

Time stood still.

Keira tried to break away.

Keira tried to break free.

And then he buried the blade into her eyeball.

NISHA

* * *

Nisha walked in through the front door of the house, and even though she couldn't explain it, she knew Keira was close.

The house was dark and smelly. It smelled really bad. Like when milk went bad, like that time when Dad didn't buy any new milk for ages and left an old bottle in the fridge, which was even worse because the fridge wasn't working anymore.

She could see things hovering above the old brown carpet. They looked like little bugs. But maybe it wasn't bugs. Maybe it was just dust. It was hard to tell. But it made her feel sneezy.

She had to be careful not to sneeze.

She didn't want anyone knowing she was here.

She walked towards the room on her right. She could smell something really bad coming from in there. It was so bad that part of her didn't want to go inside. Because part of her wanted to stay away from the bad smell.

Because it wasn't the smell of the bad people.

It was something even worse.

She could see the light. It was weird. Hard to explain. But she could *see* it, and she could *feel* it, and the voice inside her that she could feel, that was telling her to go into the room and then to—

FINISH THE JOB.

But she didn't know what it meant she didn't understand she just wanted to be okay she just wanted everything to be okay she just wanted...

She looked around.

Rufus was standing at the front door of the house. His tail was tucked between his legs. He looked scared. Like he didn't want to come inside.

And it was like he knew something bad was happening in here.

It was like he knew something bad was going to happen.

Nisha looked at him. She knew he didn't understand sign language. And she knew he didn't even like her that much.

But she signed to him.

You'll be okay. Wait.

And he looked at her. And for a minute, it was like he knew what she was saying. And like he trusted her. And that felt quite nice.

She took a deep breath of the smelly air.

She turned around.

And she walked closer and closer to the door to the smelly room.

As she got closer, she could feel her tummy tingling. Like butterflies were fluttering away in there. Only they were bad butterflies. They weren't nice butterflies at all, like the red ones that landed on her windowsill in summer sometimes, that she made friends with and gave sugar to.

They were like nasty butterflies.

No.

Not butterflies.

Bats.

She took a step closer to the room, and she put her hand on the handle, and she wasn't sure whether she wanted to open the door.

She wasn't sure if she wanted to see inside.

But she knew she had to.

She turned the handle, and she held her breath, and she tried not to think about the bats in her belly getting stronger and stronger.

Then she opened the door.

The smell hit her first. It was so bad it made her feel dizzy.

But she couldn't get too dizzy or let herself feel more sick.

Because there was something weird about this room.

There was a dinner table set. But it was all horrid and dark. And there were flies everywhere. And they kept buzzing at Nisha. Bumping into her. Headbutting her.

She looked around at the food. And the food looked bad. Like the worst food ever. Dad wasn't the best cook. But anything he cooked was better than this. Always.

People were sitting around the table. Men. Women. And a couple of children. But they weren't eating their food. Maybe they'd fallen asleep, and the flies had got their food, and that's why it smelled so bad.

But then she saw something else.

The people.

The flies buzzing around them.

The horrible little maggots crawling around them.

And...

Their eyes.

Or rather...

Where their eyes used to be.

She looked around the room at all these people without eyes.

With dark spaces where their eyes used to be.

Her heart beat faster.

Her jaw shook.

She was... scared.

Because...

She shouldn't be here.

She needed to get away from here.

Rufus was right to be scared.

It was bad here.

She turned around and went to walk out of the room when she saw something that made her freeze.

She saw a man.

She saw him holding a knife.

She saw him sitting over the top of...

Was that *Keira?*

And her mouth was moving.

And she was wriggling around underneath him. Trying to break free.

But...

Blood was oozing down her face.

And by the side of that man... right by the side of Keira...

She saw something that made her feel sick.

The man was holding a knife that was dripping with blood.

He was holding it over Keira's eye.

But the other eye...

The other eye was covered in blood.

And right beside her face...

Lying on the dirty floor...

Something that looked like a marble.

But something that wasn't a marble at all.

A bloody, creamy white marble with a black spot in the middle of it.

It wasn't a marble.

It wasn't a marble at all.

It was an eye.

It was Keira's eye.

KEIRA

* * *

If there was one thing Keira never expected to witness in her life, it was seeing her eyeball dangling from another person's fingertips.

She lay back against the hard, dusty old carpet. Splitting agony tore through the entire right side of her skull. An explosion of pain, like the worst, most crippling earache in the world, all around the inside of her head and her face. She was screaming. Or at least she was *trying* to scream. But there was a salty hand pressing over her mouth, stopping her from crying. She could feel warmth oozing down her face. She could smell it, all metallic on her top lip. Blood.

And Seth...

Seth pinned her down on the carpet.

Sliding that knife around the insides of her right eye socket.

And then, after the intense flashing lights and the splitting pain... there was darkness.

She lay on her back. She could only see through one eye. She felt like she'd been blindfolded. Or had an eyepatch placed over it.

Only... no. It was worse than that. It was different to that. There wasn't *darkness* where she once saw out of her right eye. There was...

Nothing.

And it made everything else so disorienting. In a way, it felt like she'd only ever been able to see through one eye. Through one window in her skull.

But...

Seeing him.

Holding her eyeball.

Watching him roll it to her side.

And then, seeing him perch over her with that knife hovering over her, dripping blood.

Seth looked down at her. Sweat oozed from his face and trickled down onto her. And were those... tears, too?

She looked up at him. She felt his hand pressing against her mouth. She tasted the dirt on his hand. And the sweat on his palm.

She tried to shake free of him as that burning, aching agony split even further across her head.

And then he pushed the knife against her left eye.

"I have to make you stop looking at me like that," he said, snot building at the tip of his nostril. "I have to take your eyes away. You can't look at me like that. You can't be scared. I just... I just want to be loved. All I've ever wanted is to be loved."

She lay on her back, burning with agony. And the worst thing? She actually pitied this cunt. He was a psycho. He was a murderer.

But he was actually pitiful.

How much of a mug did that make her?

But she had empathy. And she had too much empathy.

That was part of her problem.

She lay there on the floor, and she tried to pull her head back.

She tried to shift her left eye out of the way. She tried to shift herself free.

"Just stay still," he said. "Just stay still, and everything will be okay. Just stay still and..."

A smash.

A cracking smash right over Seth's head.

Blood oozed down from his skull.

She didn't know what was happening. She didn't know who this was.

But someone was here.

Someone was here, and...

Seth looked around.

And when he did, Keira saw who was right there, behind him.

"Nisha," she muttered, her mouth now free.

Nisha stood there. Holding on to a smashed plant pot. Her eyes were wide. Her hair trailed down her forehead, and her face was all greasy.

She stood there with the plant pot in her hand, and she looked at Keira like she was proud of what she'd done. But also like she wasn't sure what to do next.

And suddenly, Seth swung around at Nisha with the knife.

Keira saw her jump back. But she let out a little yelp, too. Fuck. Had he hit her? Suddenly her pity was gone. The violent bastard had swung at Nisha. Nobody fucking swung at Nisha.

Even though her head was crippled with agony, even though blood oozed down her face from her severed eyeball, she got up to her feet, and she launched across the room towards him. She went to rugby tackle him. She just had to do anything she could to knock him over, to stop him attacking Nisha.

Because she needed Nisha to be okay.

She needed Nisha to stay standing.

She needed...

And suddenly, quicker than she could process, Seth turned back around and thumped her in the face.

Hard.

And his hand. His fist.

It connected with...

Her eye socket.

Where her right eye had been severed.

Everything exploded with agony.

She lost all sense of where she was, of what was happening.

She fell back to the floor, and then the next thing she knew, she was lying there, and Seth was standing over her again, holding that knife.

Nisha right behind him.

And then she could hear...

Barking.

Barking, as Rufus came running in.

Hackles raised.

He launched himself at Seth.

And Seth swung around with the knife.

Swung it towards him.

And Keira could see it in slow motion.

She could see that knife inching closer towards his throat.

"No. Rufus. No!"

She watched it in slow motion.

Rufus.

Flying towards Seth's knife.

Nisha. Standing there. Helpless.

And Keira couldn't do anything but lie there on the floor as Seth swung the knife towards Rufus.

NISHA

* * *

Nisha saw the nasty man swinging his knife towards Rufus, and suddenly she knew she needed to do something, but she didn't know what, and she didn't know how.

Just that she had to do something.

She stood there in this dark, dusty, and smelly room. The dead people sat around the table, missing their eyes. Keira was missing an eye, too. And even though Nisha couldn't hear screaming, she was sure Keira was screaming when she first walked in.

And now she was trying to stand up. Blood falling down her face from the dark hole where her eye was missing.

And Rufus was flying through the air, his teeth on show.

Trying to get to the nasty man.

Trying to stop him from hurting Nisha or Keira.

She saw him doing this, and even though she knew Rufus didn't always like her... she knew she needed to do something.

So she closed her eyes, and she felt herself sinking into the void.

It all happened so fast.

So fast that it was hard to explain.

But she felt those bats inside her again.

She saw that darkness.

And then she saw the light.

And that light. She was holding on to that light. And she wanted to keep holding on to that light. Because if she didn't keep on holding on to that light, then something bad would happen to Keira. Because Keira was bitten. And it was only cause of the light that Keira wasn't turning into a bad person.

But...

The man.

The nasty man.

She could see him in front of her.

She could *feel* him in front of her.

And she could feel the bats all swirling around her.

All dying to get close to him.

All trying and trying to attack.

Yes dear yes don't fight it take it offer him OFFER HIM.

She swallowed a nasty taste in her mouth that was like a big lump of blood.

And then she moved into the darkness and...

KEIRA

* * *

If Keira thought she knew what was going to happen when she saw Seth swinging the blade towards Rufus's throat, she needed to remind herself that nothing quite went as she expected in this mental world.

Nothing.

Seth swung the knife towards Rufus.

Rufus hurtled across this horrible, dingy dining room towards Seth.

She watched it happening in slow motion.

Unfolding in slow motion.

She held her breath. Agony crippled the right side of her face. She could taste metallic blood all over her lips. The pain from what just happened to her eyeball—something she hadn't even had the chance to process. It was so strong. It was so intense.

But she didn't have the time to think about it.

She watched the knife inch closer and closer to Rufus. She wanted to close her eyes. She wanted to brace herself for the pain. The pain of losing someone else. Because there was nothing she could do. She didn't have the time to do anything. Not lying right here.

She watched it all unfolding in slow motion when suddenly... she looked at Nisha.

Nisha's eyes were... bleeding.

Only...

They weren't rolled back into her skull.

Not like they usually were when she entered some kind of state.

She was looking right at her.

Right in Keira's eyes.

She looked at Keira.

Blood oozing down her face.

And then she shifted her gaze to Seth.

Suddenly, Seth's knife dropped from his fingers.

His hand slumped to his side.

And *his* eyes rolled back into his head.

Keira lay there on the floor. Shaking. Rufus landed on the floor beside Seth and then ran to Keira's side, licking her face, sniffing her eyeball, then tucking himself behind her like he was waiting for something to happen. Something to unfold.

Like he was afraid.

Seth's limbs all seemed to slump. But he was still standing. His head rolled back, and blood oozed out from his ears, and then from his eyes, and then his nostrils, and his mouth. He stood there, hands stuck to his side, upright, twitching, shaking, contorting.

And Nisha stood and stared at him.

Bloodshot eyes.

Anger in her eyes.

Keira lay there and watched more and more blood ooze out from all of Seth's orifices. And even though she didn't understand exactly what was happening... she understood one thing very well. One thing in particular.

Nisha was doing this.

Whatever she was doing... she was doing it.

She thought back to the bunker. To her apology, on that note.

I've done something bad.

And it didn't make sense. Not at the time.

But all the while... Keira knew something wasn't right.

She knew right then that Nisha was holding something back from her.

And now she was witnessing it.

First hand.

Nisha couldn't just repel the infected.

She couldn't just guide the infected.

She could *cause* the infection.

And judging by what she'd done to her—the way she'd held her hand, the way the bite *hadn't* turned her... she could stop the infection, too.

Was there anything Nisha wasn't capable of?

She tried to stagger to her feet. But her head was spinning. She was dizzy. The pain in her skull, it was strong. Stronger than ever. She looked down at the musty old carpet. The blood. There was so much of it. Her eyeball. She was bleeding from her eye socket. And bleeding badly, too. No wonder she was dizzy.

She was going to pass out.

She was going to collapse.

And if she passed out and collapsed now, that would be disastrous.

She looked up. Looked up in this haze.

Seth was moving his jaw and snapping his teeth together so hard that they were beginning to crack.

Blood covered his face.

Oozed down from his mouth.

And he shook, and twisted, and contorted, and...

Turned.

She staggered to her feet when she lost her balance and tumbled over a little.

Fuck.

She was losing her balance.

She was losing her balance, and she was getting dizzier, and the pain was getting stronger, and...

She looked up at Seth and saw something different.

He wasn't shaking anymore.

He was still bleeding, sure.

But he was just standing still.

Standing still with his head rolled back, staring up at the ceiling. Eyes wide.

Like he was possessed.

She crouched there, Rufus beside her. She looked over at Nisha. She still looked in this daze. She still looked absolutely miles away.

Only...

Focused.

Focused squarely on one thing.

Seth.

"Nisha," Keira muttered. Trying to stand. And tumbling to the side again. Losing her balance. "We need to get out of here. We need... we need..."

And then she stumbled forward again.

She couldn't stand.

The dizziness was too intense.

The pain was too intense.

She stared up at Seth as he stood there, a hazy blur.

They had to get out of here.

They had to get away.

They had to...

And then, suddenly, out of nowhere...

Seth's head swung forward.

Blood trickled from his eyes.

He turned around and looked at Keira.
Then at Nisha.
With wide eyes.
Infected eyes.
And then he let out a snarl.

KEIRA

* * *

The infected Seth spun around.

He opened his mouth. Let out a shriek that sounded even more chilling than the childlike words that came out of his mouth just moments earlier.

Colours flickered in Keira's vision. She could taste blood. Her ears were ringing. Her heart was racing. She felt dizzy. She felt sick. And she was weak. So, so weak. The blood loss. The blood loss from her fucking *severed* eyeball, which still lay on the floor beside her.

Fuck. She'd had a fucking eye taken out, and she hadn't even had the chance to think about it. To process it.

'Cause she was too focused on Nisha.

On Rufus.

And now on an infected Seth, launching himself across the room towards her.

He hurtled right towards her, and Keira squeezed her eyes shut. Like that was going to do anything.

She held her breath.

She felt herself slipping.

Drifting.

She was going to pass out.

She was going to pass out, and she was going to die and...

No.

If she were going to be bitten, the infected Seth would've bitten her by now.

She opened her eyes. She didn't want to. She wasn't sure she wanted to witness her own death in slow motion.

When she opened her eyes, the infected Seth was just standing right in front of her.

Blood leaked down from both of his eyes. His eyes were bulging. Red. No... purple now.

And bulging even wider and wider.

He opened his mouth. And he made this little pitiful noise that reminded her of the Seth of old.

Almost like he was begging her.

Begging her to love him.

But when he opened his mouth, a mass of blood oozed out.

A lump of purple flesh-like meat trickled down his chin and fell onto the carpet below.

And then he screamed a gurgled cry, as a little sound exploded from his ears, and blood funneled out, and Rufus started barking, and his screaming got louder and—

A bang.

A sudden thud.

Seth's eyes.

Exploding.

Popping like balloons inside his skull.

Blood splattering all over Keira's face.

The taste of the eyeball juice trickling against her lips.

And then Seth shook, his arms rapidly vibrated, and his head darted back and forth.

And the next thing Keira knew, Seth was falling to the floor.

Shaking.

Bleeding out.

And then…

Still.

Keira looked down at Seth as he lay dead on the floor.

She looked at the puddle of blood surrounding him, which Rufus sniffed at.

And then she looked up at Nisha.

Nisha stood there. Cheeks stained in blood. Little specks of blood gathering at her chin, then dripping down to the carpet in a pitter and a patter.

Nisha looked up at her with these bloodshot eyes. As blood oozed out of her eyes, her ears, and her nostrils.

And she wanted to walk towards her.

She wanted to hold her.

She wanted to pull her close and tell her everything was okay.

She wanted to thank her.

She wanted so much to hold her right now.

But then, when she took a step towards her, the dizziness took over.

When she took a step towards her, the crippling pain at the side of her head took over.

When she stepped towards her… she tumbled forward, fell into her arms, and held her.

She held Nisha. And Nisha held her back. She could taste blood. And she could feel more and more fresh blood flowing from her severed eye.

But as she crouched there, Nisha holding her, Rufus by her side… she didn't think about the dead bodies at the table.

She didn't think about Seth's twitching corpse lying beside them all.

She didn't think of any of that at all.

She just thought of Nisha's warmth.

She just thought of Rufus's head, pressed up against her, and his wagging tail.

She just thought of Nisha and Rufus, and how hard she'd fought for them, and how they were going to be okay, and how much she'd given up for her, how much she'd fought for her, how much...

Keep her safe.

Omar's voice.

Or Jean's.

Or Dwayne's.

Or Dad's.

Or Sarah's.

Keep her safe...

She smiled.

I have.

I've kept her safe.

And she's kept me safe, too.

And then the flashing lights took over, the pain disappeared, and the warmth surrounded her.

NISHA

* * *

Nisha held onto Keira as she lay there on the floor, her body getting softer and softer and more floppy, and she didn't know what to do.

She could see the bodies all around her. The dead bodies without eyes all sitting at the table. And the body lying on the floor. The nasty man who hurt Keira. The one who took out her eye. The one who turned into a bad person before ...

Before Nisha did what she did.

She remembered the flash of light.

She remembered feeling into that light.

And then...

The dark.

She remembered falling into the dark and *feeling* the voice getting louder and louder inside her.

YES MY DEAR YES MAKE US SPREAD MAKE US GROW MAKE US...

And creeping into the nasty man's body and throwing all her

strength into making him bad, even though she didn't have much strength at all because she was weak, she was so weak.

She could taste blood. And salt, which was tears. Tears always tasted salty. She didn't know why. But she knew they were tears because she'd tasted them enough.

She stroked Keira's greasy hair with her fingers. Keira was just lying there. Lying in her arms. Still. So still. She wanted her to get up. She wanted her to wake up. Because Keira was strong. And Keira would know what to do to get out of here. To get out of this mess. She always did.

But the more she held onto Keira, the more she stroked her hair as blood trickled from her missing eyeball and onto Nisha's hand... she tasted more salt. More tears.

Because Keira wasn't waking up.

She felt a shaky hand against her neck. She thought maybe she could feel her heart beating. Or maybe feel her breathing. But she wasn't sure. She couldn't be sure. Her hands were too shaky. Everything was so shaky.

And after the last time...

After going inside the nasty man's head.

After *making* him into a bad person...

Because that's what she'd done. She could see it now.

She'd turned him into a bad person.

She was strong enough to take the bad away.

And she was strong enough to make people bad.

She felt a bit dizzy. She felt her heart racing fast. So fast that she felt like she couldn't breathe properly. Like her breaths were all hard to do. All shaky inside her.

She didn't want to be different.

She'd spent her whole life not wanting to be different.

But she *was* different.

She was different before the bad people because of her deafness.

And she was even more different now.

She held Keira tight. Squeezed her hard. People couldn't die from losing an eye, could they? But... they could die from losing blood. A lot of blood. And Keira had lost a lost of blood.

She looked around the room, and even though she was scared, she knew she needed to be strong. What would Dad do right now? That was the question she usually asked. What would Dad do?

But this time, she found herself asking something else.

What would *Keira* do?

She saw Rufus. Staring at her. Ears raised. Wagging his tail. But not like he was happy. Like he was nervous.

It's okay, she signed. Even though she was pretty sure he couldn't understand sign language. It just made her feel a bit better speaking to someone right now. *We're going to help her.*

She looked around the horrible, fly-filled room for something. She felt flies buzzing against her face. What was she looking for? Some kind of bandage. Or... alcohol. That's what people used when they were cleaning up bad wounds, wasn't it? She wasn't sure. She didn't know. She didn't want to hurt Keira more than she was already hurt. She just wanted to make her better again.

She looked all around the room, and she saw some drink on the table in front of the bodies. Some red drink. There were flies crawling all over the outside of the glass. A lot of them had fallen into the glass, too. The smell was strong. So strong.

But maybe the strong smell meant it would work better.

What was she even thinking?

It wasn't going to work. Nothing was going to work.

Because Keira was...

No!

She took a deep breath and felt sick with the smell. But she took that breath anyway, and she stood up tall like Dad had always told her to.

Stand tall.

Be strong.

She wiped the tears from her eyes and went to look in one of the other rooms for something she could use when suddenly she saw something.

Movement.

She froze.

The movement.

It was just shadows.

Outside the curtains.

Maybe... maybe someone was here to help.

Maybe she'd just imagined it.

Because she was weak. And she was tired. So maybe she'd just imagined it.

She stood there. Shaking. Her heart beating even faster now.

She had to go check.

She had to.

She stood there at the door to this horrible room that she wanted to get out of so much when she saw Rufus backing away.

Tucking his tail between his legs.

Holding back his ears.

Shaking.

Like he was scared.

She gulped.

It's okay. Don't worry.

But he still looked worried.

She stood at the door.

Looked down at Keira, lying still, blood leaking out from her eye.

She took a deep breath, and she regretted it again.

And then she turned the handle and stepped out of the door into the hallway.

She noticed two things.

First, the front door.

It was still open.

And second...

That shadow.

That shadow was approaching the door.

That shadow was getting closer.

She held her breath.

And suddenly, a grey, sore-covered, bloody hand grabbed the door and slammed it open.

They were here.

The bad people were here.

And she was too tired and weak to do anything to stop them.

NISHA

* * *

Nisha saw the bad people running into the dark house, and she felt afraid and weak.

The bad people ran down the hallway towards her. There were three of them. Or maybe more. She swore she could see more behind those at the front.

And usually, if she were feeling strong, she would've stood still. She would've tried to stay there and to stop them running towards her.

But something felt different now.

She felt weak.

She felt like... she couldn't stand in front of those bad people.

Because after what she'd done to the nasty man, she needed rest. Maybe that's how it worked. Maybe it was like when her iPad ran out of charge. She needed to charge it up again. And right now, she had no battery at all.

The horrible smell of the bad people running down the hall mixed with the horrible smells of the dead people in the room with the table and the food and the flies. But even though it smelled so bad in there, even though the thought of going back in there made her taste sick in her mouth, she knew it was all she could do.

Keira was in there.

Rufus was in there.

She needed to protect them.

She needed to be with them.

She slammed the door shut.

And then she stood there, and she knew she didn't have long. She had to push something against the door. She had to stop the bad people from getting inside.

But she didn't have much time.

She turned around. Grabbed a chair. Dragged it over. She couldn't tell if the bad people were in the room yet. One of the things with not being able to hear.

But... she couldn't *feel* the voice.

She couldn't *feel* anything.

She just had to get the chair against the door.

She just had to stop the bad people from getting inside.

She grabbed a chair, and she yanked it away from the table.

But when she pulled it... one of the dead people—an old lady with frizzy grey hair—tumbled off the table and fell onto the floor in front of her.

Loads of flies flew up in her face.

Loads of little creepy crawlies scurried around her, in and out of her eyeballs.

And the smell...

The smell was so bad.

The smell made her want to be sick.

The smell took over her.

Drowned her.

She held her breath. Tried to stop the bad smell from getting even stronger in her nose. She wished she was different right now. Why couldn't she be different right now? She'd spent her whole life not wanting to be different. But right now, she wanted to protect Keira. Right now, she wanted to protect Rufus. Right now, she wanted to...

She suddenly smelled it.

A smell.

Just a whiff in the air.

The bad people.

Then she looked around to her side.

She saw Rufus barking.

Backing away.

Running to the other side of the room.

And then she saw Keira.

Lying there.

She turned around, and she saw two bad people racing through the door, racing towards Keira.

And even though she didn't feel strong, even though she felt so weak... she saw Keira lying there.

Keira had done so much to help her.

Keira had tried so hard to save her. So many times.

Nisha might be different sometimes. She might be able to do things with the bad people that she couldn't usually do.

But, right now, she couldn't do anything like she usually could.

But that didn't mean she couldn't try.

She saw Dad in her mind.

She saw him smiling at her.

Saw him nodding at her.

And then she saw him signing.

I'm right here. Waiting for you.

And then Nisha felt a warm tear roll down her face.

I'm coming for you, she signed back.

And this time, in this moment where time stood still... in this moment where she felt so weak... she saw that Dad wasn't alone.

He was with David.

He was with Sarah.

He was with Dwayne.

He was with Beth and Kat, and he was with everyone she'd lost.

She saw them all standing there.

And then she saw Keira in front of her.

It's okay.

And then she took a deep breath, and she threw herself in front of the bad man, as he threw himself towards Keira.

It's okay, she heard.

And this time, she *did* hear it.

It was a voice.

And deep in the darkness of her mind, behind her closed eyes, she knew whose voice it was.

She knew exactly whose voice it was.

It was Dad's voice.

It's okay...

And then the bad people slammed into her.

It's...

NISHA

* * *

Nisha squeezed her eyes shut and landed in front of Keira as the bad people all flew at her, flew towards Keira, and she tried to remember how proud Dad would be of her right now for trying.

Everything was pitch black. And that was how she liked it right now. She knew that it would be pitch black for a bit. And then there might be a bit of pain. But then soon, the pain would be gone, and she'd be in heaven. She'd be in heaven, and everything would be okay.

She would be with Dad and her new friends, and everything would be okay in heaven.

The smell of the bad people and the smell of the death in the room was strong. So strong. She could taste something horrible in her mouth. Like sick.

But she didn't care.

She didn't care because she had to be strong.

For Keira.

She lay there in the darkness. And she could *feel* the bad

people getting closer towards her. And maybe she was going to be okay. Maybe she *was* still strong enough to stop them from getting her. Maybe it would work like it worked when she'd first stopped one of the bad people, Mrs Thompson, in the school toilets. She didn't think she was *doing* anything then. She just kind of... did it. As easy as moving a finger. You don't think about how you do it. You just do it.

But right now... it was kind of like she didn't even have a finger at all.

She couldn't do anything because there wasn't anything to do.

She lay there, and she tasted the tears against her lips, all salty.

Salty, like the fish and chips she and Dad used to get after they went on rollercoasters in Blackpool.

Salty like Christmas dinner and how she liked her vegetables.

Happiness.

Warmth.

She lay there, and she felt Keira. Right behind her. Keira's warmth. And even if this was the end of her life in the normal world and time for her to go to heaven... she felt... proud.

She was going to go to heaven protecting Keira.

And then she thought of something else, too.

Not just Keira. But Rufus. David. Dwayne. Sarah.

So many people.

People she'd made friends with.

New friends.

She'd spent her whole life wanting to be normal so she could make friends.

But the last however long it was, she'd been more different than ever and made the best friends she'd ever had.

She thought about Beth. The girl who she'd lost on the first day. And she felt sad. She felt so sad about losing her.

And she thought about all the other people she'd lost, too.

They didn't *need* her any different than she already was.

She didn't have to be normal.

She just had to be... her.

She felt the warmth inside her as the bad people flew at her, as they tumbled onto her, as she waited for the bites, and...

She felt the warm feeling against her face. And she realised it must be blood. It must be because she could taste it, too. So strong.

And she felt more of those bad people falling onto her.

Banging against her.

But none of them biting her.

None of them hurting her any more than a bit of weight on her.

She lay there with her eyes closed, and she held on to Keira, and she waited for the pain to fill her body.

But she didn't feel any sharp pains.

She didn't feel any teeth biting against her.

She didn't feel anything at all.

In fact... the bad people.

They had gone... still.

She lay there in the darkness. She didn't want to open her eyes. She didn't want to look.

But the longer she lay there, the more she felt like something was wrong.

She opened her eyes.

The first thing she saw was a woman. Her face was upside down. She was staring right into Nisha's eyes. She looked scary.

Nisha tried to drag herself back. She tried to get away from the lady. She was scary. Her heart was racing. She needed to get away from her. She needed to...

But then she noticed something else.

Blood.

Oozing down the lady's face.

And it didn't look like old blood.

It looked like *fresh* blood.

Why was she bleeding?

She pushed the lady away. She tried to get out of this mound of bad people, who were all still, none of them biting her.

And then she saw him.

A man.

Standing at the door.

He was wearing a mask over his mouth.

And there were two other men beside him.

Both wearing masks, too.

Both wearing army clothes.

And both holding guns.

The tall man in the middle walked into the room. He looked around. He walked slowly. She could feel the floor shaking with every heavy step.

He walked right up to her.

He crouched right down in front of her.

He looked down into her eyes with his big green ones.

And even though his mouth was covered... she swore she could see him smiling.

He held out a hand towards her.

She looked down at it.

Then around at Rufus.

Then at Keira, who lay there, still.

She looked back at the two men at the door with the guns.

Then, at the main man, holding out his hand.

She looked at his army clothes, and she saw a name stitched across it as he stood there, smiling.

The first word said *Colonel*.

And the second word was a name.

She saw his face moving. Like he was trying to speak to her. And even though normally she'd feel bad and stupid for not hearing, she didn't anymore. She lifted her fingers, and she pointed to her ears.

He looked at her for a few seconds.

And then...

And then he looked at her *bite*.

And she thought because he'd seen her bite, maybe he was going to shoot her. Maybe he was going to shoot her and then shoot Keira and then shoot Rufus and—

You don't have to worry, he signed.

He... he signed. Which meant he knew she was deaf.

And he knew how to speak to her.

I saw what you did. What you can do. We've been looking for you, he signed. *And we know how to help you. We know how you can help so, so many people.*

She saw those words forming in front of her, filling her silent world.

She saw them in front of her, moving smoother than ever before.

She remembered the last people who said she could help.

But then she saw these people, the way his arms moved, the military gear he was wearing, and the kind green eyes, and she wondered if he was different.

She needed his help.

You can help other people. You are not alone. There are others like you.

Nisha's eyes widened.

The Girl?

Leonard's eyes widened back. He paused just a second.

The Girl, he signed.

She sat there on the floor. Shaking. Covered in blood. The bad smell surrounding her.

Come on, he signed. *We can get you some place safe. You and your friends.*

She looked around at Keira. She looked dead. Nisha hoped she wasn't.

And then she looked around at Rufus. He looked scared. So scared.

She looked back at the man standing in front of her.

She looked up into his eyes.

He smiled at her.
You are okay now. You are safe now. Everything is okay now.
Nisha sat there in the middle of the mass of dead bodies.
She sat in front of Keira.
And Rufus.
She'd helped them.
She'd protected them.
Just like they protected her so many times.
Now, it was their turn to be helped.
She took another deep breath of the horrible, smelly air.
And then she reached up a hand and took his hand.
He tightened his grip around her hand.
Stroked it, just slightly.
His smiling eyes widened even more.
You're going to be okay now...
She thought about that name as she took his hand.
Everything is going to be okay now, he signed.
He could hardly stop the smile creeping up his face.
Colonel Leonard Hartwell.

SARAH

* * *

Sarah stared down the road.

The sun beamed down from above. Her skin tingled with warmth. Her heart raced. If it beat any faster, it felt like it might just burst inside her chest. Break out, like the alien in that eighties movie. Or was it a seventies movie? Did it even matter right now?

The road was silent. Birds singing above. Crows. Their singing echoing around the road.

The smell of blood lingering in Sarah's nostrils.

And the *taste* of it, too, across her dry lips.

She looked across the road. She should be dead. The infected. They were all racing towards her. Towards this military vehicle she was on. Which had now broken down.

They should've reached her.

They should've killed her.

All of them should've swarmed her, and she should be dead.

But she wasn't dead.

She was alive.

And the infected...

They were all standing opposite her.

They were all still.

Totally still.

The ones in front of her.

The ones behind her.

Totally still.

She looked around at them.

Looked at them all.

Why weren't they coming for her?

Why weren't they attacking her?

What was happening?

She looked into the eyes of a young ginger boy, who stood there and shook violently. A woman, grey-skinned, blood-tinged vomit trickling down her chin.

There had to be someone close. Someone like Nisha. Someone like Carly. That was the only explanation for it. It *had* to be.

But there was nobody.

There was only her.

She stood there. Her heart pounded. She couldn't stop thinking about what Carly told her. The last thing she'd told her, before she died.

And she couldn't stop thinking of what it meant.

For her.

For Nisha.

For the future.

She felt the pain in her back.

She remembered the trip to the hospital when she passed out.

Insisting she just had a bad back. That she'd had spinal issues all her life, ever since her fall.

She remembered the scan.

She remembered the doctor's words.

I'm sorry, Sarah. It's cancer. And it's terminal. There is nothing we can do...

She thought about Carly and her final words.

I have cancer. That's what stops them. That's what holds them back. That's... Mother.

And she looked at the crowd of infected, standing right in front of her.

They weren't attacking.

She took a deep breath.

A tear rolled down her face.

She couldn't deny it anymore.

But the death sentence she'd received was the reason she was still alive.

END OF BOOK 7

Beyond Salvation, the eighth book in The Infected Chronicles series, is now available.

If you want to be notified when Ryan Casey's next novel is released—and receive an exclusive post apocalyptic novel totally free—sign up for the author newsletter: ryancaseybooks.com/fanclub